THE EX-MAS DUET

Copy Editor / Line Editor / Proofreader: Cassidy Hudspeth Edits

Cover Design: BooksAndMoods

Formatting: Grace Elena Formatting

To my songbirds.
Keep writing from the heart, no matter what.

Author's Note

This is a standalone holiday novella set apart from the Tennessee Roots Universe (Alpine Ridge series, etc).

Ever since attending Belmont University in Nashville, TN and being surrounded by such inspirational songbirds, I've always wanted to write a songwriting MC. This might not be my Opry debut, Dad, but it's my own version.

I hope you enjoy this piece of me that I've kept hidden for a while. The original song lyrics that I wrote for this book will be at the end.

Grace Elena 🖤

Content Warnings

This novella is suited for readers 18+.

The following content warnings are: low spice and explicit sexual scenes, drinking, cursing, and mental health topics such as anxiety.

Playlist

Blue Christmas - Megan Moroney
Fade Into You - Sam Palladio, Clare Bowen
Mustand or Me - Megan Moroney
Hey Highway - Hannah McFarland
Strangers - Kameron Marlowe, Ella Langley
Tin Man - Miranda Lambert
Heroin - Jessie Murph
Blues, You're A Buzzkill - Miranda Lambert
people change - Ella Langley
Wonder - Megan Moroney
Devil Don't Go There - Lainey Wilson
I Hate This - Tenille Arts
Sip - Jessie Murph
Bad As The Rest - Jessie Murph
Come Over (Acoustic Mixtape) - Sam Hunt
Hell At Night - BigXthaPlug, Ella Langley

2016 - Sam Hunt
Man of the Year - Sam Barber
Whiskey Into Water - Hannah McFarland
Strangers - Ashley Cooke, Daniel Kim Ethridge
Opposite of Love - Ashley Cooke
Turned Into Missing You - Max McNown, Avery Anna
Forever Ain't Long Enough - Max McNown
Let The Lonely - Kameron Marlowe
Backwards - Jonas Brothers
Mess With Missing You - Jordan Davis, Carly Pearce
Ain't Enough Road - Jordan Davis
Wi$h Li$t - Taylor Swift
Opalite - Taylor Swift
everytime - Ariana Grande
Feelings - Hunter Hayes
Broken Hearts Break - Hannah McFarland
Get Back - Demi Lovato
Don't Mind If I Do - Riley Green, Ella Langley
I'll Find You - 5 Seconds of Summer

Paloma

CHAPTER ONE

THE CRUMPLED paper stares back at me like a dagger through the heart. There's no blood—there doesn't need to be. I still feel the effects of it as my eyes linger. I could walk away, but the pain keeps me grounded.

A hint of handwritten lyrics peek through the edges, and *you tried* is visible, creating a weight in my chest.

A knock at the door makes me jump and I kick the paper, letting it roll under the coffee table. I sniffle a bit, getting up and heading out of the living room to the foyer. There's a mirror I pass, doing a quick pitstop to make sure there's no mascara that accidentally smeared. I'm all in one piece, as I should be.

My lips turn into a scowl the moment I swing the door open and see my manager, Montrose Wright, smiling brightly. There's no reason for him to be cheesing that wide, like the Cheshire cat; it makes my blood boil a bit.

His smile fades as he takes a step forward, but I keep myself planted in the entryway. "What's wrong, Paloma? You're not happy to see your favorite person?"

"Not after that last meeting," I confide, finally taking a step back to let him inside.

He clears his throat as he digs his hands in the pockets of his jeans and looks around the place. I started to decorate a bit for the holidays, but I gave up halfway. It's evident he can see it with the way his eyes scan the living room and notices half of the tree standing tall and the upper part haphazardly on the floor. My best friend and roommate, Lacey, gladly lets me decorate, but it's never gotten this bad where I can't finish.

"Glad to see you're at least in a jolly spirit," he notes. I roll my eyes and head back to the living room to plop on the white couch, kicking my feet up on the coffee table. The crumpled paper burns through the ground as I stare at it again.

"What's jolly about being told none of your new songs are good?" I pout. The meeting replays in my mind, and I want to grab a pillow and scream into it.

Montrose rounds the corner and sits on the chair across from the couch. He leans in, elbows propped on his knees. His blue eyes are staring into my soul, but I refuse to let him pry. I focus instead on his graying beard and buzzcut that he swears he will grow out one day. That was a promise he made three years ago.

The crow's feet increase as he narrows his eyes, and I finally sigh, looking at him. "Listen, I talked to the label and they want a few more songs to hear. You can do that, right?"

"The last five took me months to write. I can't whip something out of thin air to give them by next week, let alone *a few more*," I confess. Montrose knows better than anyone that my career has been on the line, and I'm doing my best. I can't write like I used to anymore. I get by with a hit single every couple months, but that's not enough for a demanding label that prides themselves on bestselling songwriters and country artists.

If I can't give them hit after hit like I used to, then I'm useless. The spark I once had is getting harder and harder to find. I have a guitar case full of unfinished songs, melodies that never got written, and duet sheets that will never see the light of day.

Montrose leans even further and taps my leg that's

outstretched on the coffee table. I focus back on our conversation and give him a small smile before shrugging.

"You can do it. I believe in you," he finally says.

I laugh. "That's as encouraging as the label's unsaid promise of hacking my career if I don't deliver."

I pull my legs off the coffee table, his hand dropping. I get up and head to the mantle where a tiny reindeer figurine sits. My mom got it for me when I was ten one Christmas. I called him Ferris, because, of course, you give everything that looks cute a name when you're younger. I stare at Ferris, hoping he can tell Santa I need a Christmas miracle.

"They won't fire you. You have a contract," Montrose reminds me of the inevitable. A once five-year contract is coming to an end very soon and *then* they'll be able to get rid of me.

I'll just be another washed-up songwriter off Music Row, just like my father. How comical is that?

"Maybe I can hide away in the mountains and wait it out," I joke, taking my eyes off Ferris and raising my brow at Montrose. His expression is blank before his eyes narrow and brows pinch together. *Oops.*

"That's the last thing you'll do, Paloma. As your manager, I have the duty to not only make sure you're on the right track and protect your intellectual property, but also make sure you don't go off the deep end."

I sigh. "I'm not going off the deep end. I'm just simply *disappearing* from the label so the contract can end and I can be free."

Montrose looks at me for a moment, his eyes and shoulders relaxing in the way they do when he tries to understand me. He reminds me of my father when he's in this state.

"I can't let you do that, personally," he starts. "I care about you, Paloma, and you know it. How about we table this until tomorrow? But think about it, please?"

There's silence for a bit until I move closer to him. He stands and brushes off any wrinkles from his pants. A routine I know so well, having worked with him for all these years.

"Do you really think I could pull it off?" I ask, my voice fading as I'm deep in thought. I gather the next few words carefully. "Montrose…I can't write like I used to because I'm half of a whole now. I can't function as a solo songwriter like I thought I could."

He's quiet for a moment before he steps closer and lays a hand on my shoulder, squeezing lightly. "I've seen how you rise from the ashes. Your works are incredible as a solo songwriter, Paloma. You doubt yourself too much."

His words comfort me for a moment before the self-doubt fills my head, and I let it wrap its arms around me, pulling me into a comfortable embrace.

"I guess I'll grab my guitar and journal," I whisper, and Montrose smiles, patting my shoulder before stepping back and heading toward the front door. I don't follow him, but I give a small wave. The front door clicks closed and I let out a deep breath.

I'm not sure why I lied to him. All the songs I've been giving my label have been ones written before things took a turn. In truth, I haven't written in *months*.

I'm screwed.

Graham

CHAPTER TWO

I SHOULD JUST DELETE my dating apps, for fucks sake.

> JENNA
> Bet you could write a song about how good I
> treat you in bed.

That message was the last straw before I deleted the account. And then I proceeded to do it for the rest of them I was registered for. I don't even know why I was on the damn things—I wasn't entertaining the conversations as much as I thought I would and the dates I'd tried were all full of self-absorbed country artist wannabes trying to fit their shoes in the scene by getting close to me.

It felt like I was just a stepping stone to someone else's career, if there was even one to begin with. My best friend and roommate, Stetson Brooks, would claim I need to stop swiping on girls who had *your next favorite country singer* in their bio. I just wanted to see if I could connect with someone who shared the same passion.

Never again.

"You're up early." Stetson's voice makes me jump as he

enters the kitchen and yawns, shaking his head wildly, his long black hair moving with it. I grunt, staring at the now-empty folder in my phone that held the god-forsaken apps.

He is loud as he opens and closes cabinets and the fridge to get cereal and milk, his tall figure prominent in my peripheral. His daily routine of Trix with way too much milk is something I'll always like about him. He's a kid at heart and reminds me of our good ol' days in middle school when we met.

The milk spills over the rim as he slams the bowl on the table and takes a seat. I finally give him a disapproving look. "I just cleaned the table."

Stetson looks at the spill before twisting the corner of his mouth and pulling a napkin from the stack we leave for instances like this. "My bad, man. Long night with—"

"Is it Leslie this time? Or Jade? Wait, no, Taylor?" I start calling off the names of the many girls he has been stringing along this month. As much as I love Stetson, he is a player, and I make sure to remind him every single second of every day. Gotta keep him humble somehow.

He rolls his eyes as he eats a big spoonful of cereal. "Leslie is on vacation with her family at the beach, and Jade said she wanted exclusivity, so we broke things off. I have no idea about Taylor, to be honest. How's your dusty roster?"

"Still gathering dust," I quip. I wave my phone to him. "Just deleted the damn apps. Got tired of the fakeness and only wanting me for one thing."

"Not two things?" he jokes before eating another spoonful. I raise a brow before grunting again.

"Nashville girls only want to be at the top. They don't know what it's actually like once you're there. Franklin girls are worse."

"You'd know," Stetson confirms.

I shrug, not wanting to think too much of my prime as one of the best solo songwriters in Nashville. He's no stranger to it either, with his family roots. Once the girls in this industry find out you're well known, they'll do anything to get close to you for their career's benefit.

"They need a reality check, is all," I say, softer this time. "I don't want to be that for them anymore."

Stetson is quick to finish his bowl before giving me a nod. "I can introduce you to a few of my musician friends if you need someone down to Earth. Hell, maybe Colbie knows some nice girls."

The idea of him asking his very famous country superstar older sister, Colbie Brooks, makes my body visibly shudder. "I don't think moving from country singer wannabes to musicians is calling it *down to Earth*. I think moving to a different playing field would be better."

"Like what?"

I think about it. "Teacher? Social Worker? Someone who works at a dog shelter? That type."

Stetson laughs as his chair scrapes back. "Yeah, that's so *you*. You need someone who understands your lyrical mind. You need someone like—"

I push my own chair back and get up. "No, Stetson."

"What? I didn't even say her name. Jesus."

There's nothing I'd like more to do than not think about *her*. I head to the back door and grab the keys to my Colorado. Stetson finishes washing his plate and gives me a look. A pained one.

"That was a thing of the past. I've moved on and so should you," I retort.

"I can't really 'move on' from my cousin's best friend, but fine, I'll drop it," he replies, his fingers going up in quotations.

Just another reminder that she'll always be in my life, no matter how hard I try to keep the distance. Paloma didn't move to Nashville to follow her best friend Lacey until we were in our early twenties. The normal age for dreamers to get a head start in their careers in this city. Lacey, of course, wanted to be taken seriously in the wine bar business, so her ties with Stetson and Colbie have always been more familial than professional—as they should be.

Thinking back to those years of younger me feels like I'm reliving memories from someone I no longer recognize. That isn't who I am anymore, but I'm still dealing with the aftermath of his actions.

"Heading to work?" he calls out behind me. I nod and throw my hand up with two fingers sticking out as a salute before I head out the door and get in my truck.

The radio starts playing a song from another record label that tried to buy a few demos from me, but I gave them a hard no. They have amazing songwriters, a few of them I've had the pleasure of working with, so I didn't want to get in their way. Younger me would've taken the opportunity, but I can't do that anymore.

It doesn't feel right stepping back into those shoes I've once burned and charred.

And now one of our favorite songs from long ago is charting again, so why not refresh your memories? Here's Needing You Like This *by Colbie Brooks and Irving Holland.*

I switch off the radio as quickly as possible, the knob feeling like lava under my fingertips. That fucking song always comes on the damn radio when I least need it.

My phone vibrates and I look at it to see Stetson's text. I quickly glance up at the house, but he's not creepily peeking through any of the blinds like I suspected him to.

STETSON

She's really showing up today.

I roll my eyes and grunt before typing out a response.

ME

I blame you for even trying to speak her name
into existence. You listening in?

STETSON

Always, it's one of my favorite songs.

ME

You have bad taste.

STETSON

First off, ouch. That's my sister. Second, y'all
won a fucking grammy for this song.

The three little dots in a bubble pop up and I gnaw at my lip
with my teeth. The low blow wasn't my aim, but it's said and
done.

STETSON

You could win another if you just stopped
feeling sorry for yourself.

I laugh, feeling like a crazy person sitting in my truck. My
emotions are all over the place, and the cause is the lyrics
playing on the radio right now. My fingers are quick to type out a
response, and before I can think, my thumb hits send.

ME

I didn't mean that, Stets, you know it. Sorry.
But that's not what I'm doing. Plus, we didn't
win the grammy, it was for record of the year.
Not song of the year. We just get credit in their
speech. You should know this.

STETSON

Colbie doesn't explain the nitty gritty to me
when she accepts Grammy's. It's a damn
good song and not just because she sang it.
The ones who wrote it hold the power in this
case.

ME

Thanks. See you at Sparrow's tonight?

STETSON

you got it.

I toss my phone in the cup holder before backing out of the driveway and head to one of my favorite coffee shops to get my morning started. I have a few meetings with my manager and label, which apparently is super important and I have to be fully alert for—hence the coffee I desperately need. Then I have a spot tonight at Sparrow's for their open mic night, where a few of us songwriters play a few originals. It's a place to be discovered and where I got my start.

It feels nice to return there after everything. To be surrounded by like-minded artists and hear words that fill your soul with purpose.

I have a new original I've been working on, not for work, but for myself, that I want to play tonight. It's in my guitar case in the backseat, a habit I've yet to kick and will soon learn my lesson the day a window is broken into and the case is missing.

By the time I get my coffee and park, there's a bustling crowd on Music Row, the stretch of blocks that house publishing and recording studios like a stack of dominoes. Tourists with maps and workers heading to their offices, as I head to the front doors of my label's building. The tiny publishing house I work under, Indigo Roots, is right next to the egregious building in a cute cottage home and a place I'd rather be on any given day.

With one tiny glance at the house, I head into the building and make my way to the elevators that take me to the tenth floor, where my manager is waiting for me.

"You're early," Montrose Wright calls out with a big smile. I give him one back before we close the distance and I hand him the small coffee I got for him. He seems grateful to grab it, and we start walking toward the back of the space where the conference room is.

"So what's this meeting about? Got anything to prep me?"

Montrose walks slower and I mimic his pace, albeit being a few inches taller than him, so it feels funny. He gives me a look, and I raise a brow.

"You're not going to like this, Graham—"

"What do you mean?" I ask, wanting to halt our steps, but the clock is ticking, and Montrose hates being late.

"I should've called you last night, but things have been so hectic," he confesses, and my mind is running a mile a minute trying to decipher what this meeting could entail.

We reach the conference room doors, and Montrose gives me one last pitiful look before opening one side for me.

I almost trip into the room the moment I take a step. Everything in me screams to run away and never look back. To pack my guitar and hightail it to the furthest point of the world. That's all I need, my guitar and my voice.

Because not only is the head of the label at the table, but I lock eyes with the only person in the world that can still make my heart skip mid-beat.

Paloma Gentry-Tapia.

Paloma

CHAPTER THREE

THIS CAN'T BE HAPPENING.

I look at Montrose from the entrance of the conference room and cock my head slightly. His eyes glance from Graham to me, his lips twisting into a pained curve, and I can tell this is the hardest thing he's had to do in his career.

Because how the hell do you continue to manage your best songwriters after they break up, let alone work under the same label? Our meetings haven't overlapped since—

"So glad you can join us," Loren, the CEO, speaks up from her seat. There are three other people with her, sitting across the conference table from me: the A&R director, marketing director, and music attorney. I got here early, as usual, so I already made small talk with them.

Graham is usually early, but today he's cutting it close. It makes me wonder why, but I have to stop my thought process from caring too much. I'm not owed any explanation… anymore.

Loren's bright, red hair falls into priceless curls as she studies Graham and Montrose, who finally cross the room to their seats. Montrose makes sure to sit between us, and I send a silent thanks to the man upstairs.

Her green eyes study us three for a few more seconds, the silence becoming more prominent than the elephant in the room. Graham clears his throat and I turn to look.

He's got a five o'clock shadow now and his eyes look tired. Hell, all of him looks tired. Must be *so* tiring being a successful songwriter.

"We're ready," Montrose speaks up, glancing at both of us. I give a small nod, but Graham keeps his head straight.

Loren looks at her team, who shuffle a few papers across the table to her. "We've got a proposal for Paloma and Graham."

She doesn't use our last names. She doesn't separate us. Her words are conjoined, as if what was, *is*.

"We're listening," Montrose speaks for us again. I know he knows a bit about what's going on today, but he couldn't give me any details. I just know that this meeting will spare me. It's my "lifeline" as Montrose said over the phone yesterday.

Loren talks about metrics for a bit and stats of the company, highlighting where they've been able to stay on top as country music's number one record label. And then she proceeds to go into the stats of the relevant things: how we're still one of the best labels with publishing houses that produce the best songwriters in Nashville, if not the country.

Indigo Roots has been my home for so many years that I sometimes forget we're under the umbrella of Brooks Row Records.

Graham shifts in his seat and I swear I can hear every sound from this man, no matter how hard I try to tune him out. My skin is crawling with nerves and I begin to chew on the inside of my cheeks. I cross my arms over my chest and lean back a bit against my chair.

"Colbie Brooks is requesting five songs from you," Loren

finishes. I immediately straighten in my seat and look at her incredulously.

Colbie Brooks has been the biggest country artist for the last decade and she gave Graham and me our break when she chose our first written duet years ago. It felt like a whirlwind, thinking back to how much I thought I could get after that. That "break" I got was being able to sign a five-year contract to secure a spot with my label. But I never really got a break like Graham did.

The fact that *she* wants me to write for her again? Is this finally *my* break?

"I'm sorry, did you say Colbie Brooks?" I slip out, not realizing that it just came out of my mouth. My eyes widen and I snap my head to Montrose, who gives me a small smile. Okay, I didn't fuck this up. Although my best friend is her cousin, they don't really talk music and *we* barely talk about the Brooks family. It's kind of like *Fight Club*, you don't talk about it. I have nothing but professional respect for Colbie and I want to keep it that way.

Loren smiles and even chuckles. The three men next to her do the same and I don't feel like I'm on a chopping block anymore. "Yes, Colbie would love to have you write a few songs for her. She's thinking of a Christmas EP to fast release."

Graham is the next one to speak up. "I've got a few demos she can listen to."

"Me too," I say, knowing I have at least one Christmas-esque lyric sheet in my guitar from way back.

Loren laughs and shakes her head. "No, I don't think I was clear with the request."

My brows pinch together and I look around the room. "She wants us to write a song? We have songs for her," I say.

"I probably have all the songs she needs," Graham adds, and my stomach drops. My breathing begins to slow and it feels slightly heavier around my chest. Like something is sitting on top of it. I try to take a big breath in and blow a big one out.

Montrose raps his knuckles on the conference table. "I think what Loren is saying is that Colbie Brooks would like songs from *both* of you. Ones that you've written together."

There's silence. The knife digs an inch deeper as each second passes. The one holding it turns to look at me.

"I'm not sure if Montrose told you, but we don't write together anymore."

Montrose shifts in his seat and clears his throat. If he had a tie on, I bet he'd be twisting it in his hands right now.

"I wasn't aware," Loren states. She doesn't say anything else, and my heart skips a beat. Fuck.

"I—I think what Graham is saying is that—" I start, my throat dry and I cough before continuing, "we haven't written in a while, so we're rusty."

Graham clicks his tongue against his teeth and his jaw ticks.

Loren looks at the men at the table who've remained quiet before telling them to leave the room. My hands get clammy and it feels like my throat has officially closed. Everything is starting to close in on me. The lights in this room are starting to blind me and the air feels thicker. I'm dying, that's what's happening. Right?

"This has been sprung on them out of nowhere, Loren," Montrose attempts to start, but Loren raises her hand. He shuts up immediately. I don't even want to attempt to speak, or else I know I'll be packing my things from Indigo Roots and booking it out of Nashville.

Her green eyes are determined and the next few words out of her mouth make me want to throw up. "Colbie Brooks isn't someone you say no to, especially when it comes to the songwriters at this record label. I pride this company on collaboration and ultimately, honesty. We do our best on the business aspect to be honest with our artists and anyone else who is employed. I'd like the same in return. So, tell me, why am I getting push back?"

The moment Graham starts to speak, I'm transported back to the past, recalling how he always spoke for us in meetings and negotiations. He would even do his best to be the face of our duet "brand" and show up solo to meetings if I was too in my head and couldn't face the label. He always had my back, but he shouldn't right now. It confuses me.

"We haven't worked together for over three years. We stopped writing together two years ago. We're not *just* rusty, we're no longer compatible to write for an artist who'll need the songs in a quick turnaround."

His words are worse than a knife. It cuts deep into my soul and I try to hold back tears. I close my eyes for a few seconds and uncross my arms, letting them fall on my lap. I look at Loren, who is focused on Graham, as my right fingers begin tapping the side of my left hand. Something my therapist taught me to try whenever things get too much.

She finally looks at me, raising a brow. I tap a few more times before gaining the courage to speak. "I'm sure there are plenty of current duet songwriters who will be a much better fit than us."

"Colbie specifically asked for you two. Paloma and Graham. Not anyone else."

"Graham made a good point about writing again in a quick fashion. Songs take time; we wouldn't be able to finish when she'd need them to record."

The lie falls from my lips so easily. Loren doesn't seem fazed, but she also doesn't seem to know the absolute lie it was. Songwriters can write something in ten minutes if they're really in their heads about it. Our smash hit duet song was written in thirty minutes… Okay, it was written in two hours with a few breaks in between, but the details don't matter.

"What's the barrier?" Loren asks us both. I let Graham take the wheel and he thankfully does.

"I've got some gigs at Sparrow's I can't get out of. Personal things, too."

"Yeah," I chime in.

Loren laughs and shakes her head. Montrose has been silent this whole time, but he drops his head like a disappointed father.

"I'm sure Sparrow's can miss you for a few days. You're not new to adjusting your personal life to fit in clients that need work done."

She's not wrong about that. My teeth pull my bottom lip and I begin to chew.

"And you? You have gigs at Sparrow's?"

I gulp. "No, ma'am. It's just the quick turnaround needed that I'm worried about. Even if we rescheduled things to find time to write, it takes time to get back into the process. To get back to the mindset and environment to knock out a lot of songs."

Loren takes in my words, and I appreciate her silence for once. She looks from me to Graham and nods. She places her hands on the table and slides her chair back before standing. Her gaze moves to Montrose.

"There are a few things I'll have to finalize, but I'll keep in touch with you today about this."

"Yes, ma'am," Montrose replies, standing up as well. He looks at me and raises a brow, and I immediately follow cue and stand beside him. Graham remains seated.

Loren eyes me. "Will I be able to tell Colbie that you're good to go?"

It takes me a bit to agree, but the only thing holding me back is having to spend my days and possibly evenings with Graham at Indigo Roots. I'd rather touch a hot stove and burn my fingertips so I can't play guitar anymore than get stuck in a studio with him again.

But in reality, I can do it. I can suck it up. I don't have any plans this week, unless you count the self-loathing and pity party I throw for myself every night at 9 p.m. on the dot.

"Yes," I finally blurt.

Graham chuckles and I snap my head toward him, throwing daggers with my eyes. He doesn't even glance in my direction before he stands up and crosses his arms over his chest. "Sure, but can't promise those songs will be ready in time. Tell her that."

Loren blinks, opening her mouth, and it scares the shit out of me to see what she'd say. Graham is being completely unprofessional right now with the CEO of our label. But he doesn't have much hanging on the line for him like I do. He can sacrifice this job if he truly needs to.

The contract end date looms over me like a cloud, and I'm starting to feel a drizzle.

"I'll call you around noon," Loren tells Montrose before walking out.

It's silent as the conference door closes before Montrose steps back to look at us both. Graham finally turns to me, and I have to look away, keeping my eyes on my shoes. Anywhere but him.

That's when Montrose speaks up. "What the fuck was that, you two?"

Graham

CHAPTER FOUR

SHE BRINGS the worst out of me. She really does.

Or at least that's what I'm trying to convince myself right now as Montrose gawks at us.

What the fuck was that, you two? His words are sharp and I know I'm the one to blame. I could've jeopardized everything with the shit I just pulled with Loren. I'm not sure what possessed me to behave the way I did in front of her…

The ghost of exes past, most likely.

Montrose is waiting for one of us to speak, but we're silent. It's quieter than the last night I spent with Paloma years ago.

I'm about to speak up when Montrose shakes his head and waves his hand at us both in disappointment. He turns and heads to the conference doors and pulls them open—that's when Paloma lets out a noise.

"I'll do it, no matter what," she proclaims. Her brown eyes are wild like she's got something stirring her thoughts, but I can't allow myself to care what it could be.

Montrose looks back at her and his lips turn into a frown before he responds. "With the way things are, Paloma, you really have no choice."

Before she can say anything, he leaves, and the doors are loud behind him. We're left in this room, his words remaining in the air like stuffy humidity sticking to your skin.

Paloma is biting her lip, and I begin to feel bad. What did Montrose mean by that? She already said yes to Loren, so I wasn't expecting her to drill it into Montrose.

"Everything okay?" The words slip out before I can shut up. She glances up at me and her cheeks redden, the way they usually do. She's gotten a little paler from the fall weather, but she's still got the same way about her. The Paloma I used to know every inch of.

"Y-yeah, why?"

"I don't know… Doesn't seem like it," I let out slowly. She nods quickly before sidestepping me to get to the conference doors. I rush ahead of her to open them—it's the least I can do. She gives me a small smile before slipping past me.

"I guess I'll see you around," she almost whispers, giving me one more glance before she nearly bolts down the hallway to the elevators.

I don't get the chance to respond to her, but the words hang off my lips.

"Yeah, you too," I whisper, watching her go. The image before me is a stark reminder of what I saw years ago.

When I broke Paloma's heart.

"I'M GRAHAM WESTIN, I've been writing since as long as I can remember," I speak into the mic while strumming my guitar. The crowd is small, but that's what I love the most about Sparrow's.

You can play your songs here during their songwriting rounds and get your start, or you can simply come and play without worrying about your fame status. I've heard Irving play here multiple times over the last few years, amongst other amazing artists who have sung my songs.

"This is a new one," I continue, clearing my throat. "I've kind of been in a rut lately, trying to figure out my voice again. Ever feel that way? Life knocks you down and you forget who you are as a writer…"

There are a few nods around the room, and I continue to strum a few chords before giving them a nod. "It's a little rusty, but here goes. It's called *Tennessee Smokeshow.*"

I start strumming more chords and picking at the strings before singing the first verse. It captivates the audience almost immediately, and the feeling in my chest is tight, but in a familiar way. It's emotional, baring your soul to strangers, but I love it. Being able to see people I don't know relate to lyrics and a story that I once walked. Or in this case, a path I'm still strutting down.

The chorus comes quickly and there's already a few people swaying to the words.

I've got a few words for you, darling
Don't take this for granted
What happened to your eyes sparkling
It's what got me enchanted
You're a Tennessee Smokeshow, baby
Radiant piece of art
You're a Tennessee Smokeshow, baby
That's from my heart

I go into a few more verses and a chorus again, then sing a bridge, and end on another chorus. I strum one last chord before looking up, already forgetting I was at Sparrow's with a live audience. My mind brought me back to my living room and being alone. My secret garden.

The audience claps wildly with a few hollers, and I look out to see Stetson in the corner, raising his beer to me. A smile splits my face as I thank the listeners, before putting down my guitar and allowing the next artist to start their intro.

My heart is still pumping loudly in my ears, the spiraling thoughts starting to take over my mind and drowning out the person next to me talking. Did people really like this song? Or did they just clap because they were being nice?

I try not to focus on the thoughts, but they're loud. I stay in this trance for a moment before realizing the person has finished singing their whole song, and the crowd starts clapping. I shake my head slightly, trying to refocus. It's been a while since I've allowed the thoughts to take over like that, but damn, that was something.

Did anyone notice? I congratulate the artists, words coming out of my mouth as I shake hands and pack my guitar. That's when I feel a pat on my back and let out a breath of relief to see Stetson with his wide eyes.

"You killed it, man. I forgot how great of a lyricist you are." He smiles.

"Jeez, thanks," I chuckle. He grabs my guitar case from me and nods over his shoulder.

"Wanna grab more beers for us while I put this in the back with Baxter?" He's the owner of the cafe and sometimes lets us store our equipment in his office if we plan to stay longer than the open mic night.

I nod. "Sure, thanks, man."

I watch Stetson walk to the back, and a few people come up to me to thank me for singing. There's an older man who lets me know he's missed seeing me play here. It warms my heart knowing I still have my people here who welcome me with open arms, no matter how far I wander.

Once I get us a few beers, I head to a vacant bar table and set them there before Stetson rejoins me. He's got a giddy smile on his face, and I raise a brow.

"You alright?"

He nods. "I just got a text from Colbie."

My ears perk up at this. The day was a whirlwind, not just the morning meeting with Loren, but also another meeting with Montrose in the early afternoon to solidify some plans for the request. I had to sign a few things as well.

"Yeah, you know it was too good an offer to say no to," I gently let out. I don't want to really talk about his sister and business, but he's my best friend and I'm sure he just wants to get updates.

"She mentioned it's with—"

I take a quick pull of my beer and let it sit in my mouth for a second, relishing in the taste before swallowing. Stetson looks at me for a moment. I set the glass down a little harder than necessary.

"If I could do it without her, I would," I finally say.

"Ouch," he replies instantly. The words I just let out sting, but I can't take them back. I try not to downplay my emotions around Stetson. We all need someone in our lives that we can be wholeheartedly truthful to. That's him for me.

"I just can't imagine being in a room with her for that many hours; it's been so long." Memories of our writing times fill my vision, the way we'd stay up hours even past closing just to make sure we got a song finished. Paloma filled my days and nights so effortlessly. Now, having to think that we'll be doing that all over again for Colbie's EP stirs something heavy in my stomach.

Stetson pulls his beer to his lips before taking a sip and locking eyes with me. "Do you ever think about the days you did write with her? And were together?"

I swallow the thick cotton that's somehow lodged in my throat, pushing the sudden memories away and trying to focus on the present with Stetson. "Sometimes."

He raises a brow. I roll my eyes.

"*Okay*, more than sometimes. But there's nothing I can do.

What's said and done and I'm sure she can say the same. Probably worse, even."

"Well," he starts, "how did this morning go? Do you have any battle scars?"

I hesitate for a moment, wanting to bite back at him, but I take a deep breath instead. "No, we didn't fight or argue. Actually, I kind of was a jackass throughout the whole meeting and barely looked her in the eyes."

"That's tough."

I nod, taking another long pull of my beer. I look around the dwindling crowd at Sparrow's as people start to leave for their nightly plans. My phone buzzes and I pull it out, glancing at the text notification preview.

MONTROSE THE MAN

All writing rooms are booked out for the remainder of the month, even other houses can't give us a space.

I glance at Stetson, who raises a brow, and I sigh, finally opening the text thread and typing out a reply. "Seems like things are about to get a whole lot more complicated," I say to Stetson.

ME

So, we write at cafes or what?

MONTROSE THE MAN

Not exactly. You'll need to pack a bag.

My brows furrow. "What's going on?" Stetson asks. I shrug before rubbing my hand over my chin.

"All writing spaces are booked. Think they're gonna rent out a hotel room or something for us to go to. Conference room? I have no clue."

Stetson laughs and I give him a glare. "That'll really make her hate you, huh?"

"As long as I can go back to my own bed every night, I'm fine with whatever ends up working out," I say before resuming typing.

ME

Don't think I'll need a bag for a few hours a day in a hotel.

Montrose is typing, and the three-dot bubble shows for a bit before his text comes through. The moment I read it, my breath falters, and my chest feels heavy.

MONTROSE THE MAN

You'll get your own room, but the label will be renting out a hotel room for your songwriting with Paloma to make sure this gets completed in a timely manner. So pack for at least five days.

"Five days?!" It comes out louder than I expect, and Stetson finally scoots his chair closer to me and reads over my shoulder. He huffs out a breath.

"Shit, man. Guess you'll be going to your *hotel* bed every night. At least you won't need to share it with anyone." I give him a side-glare. "What? Think of this as a work trip!"

"This feels like a mandated school trip with chaperones," I mutter before texting *okay* to Montrose. Whatever, the week will fly by and I'll dish out whatever songs Colbie needs.

It'll be quick and easy. I'll give her the damn Christmas songs she needs like I'm ripping off a bandaid.

"Maybe you and Paloma will leave as friends," Stetson says, patting my back before he scoots his chair back to its original position.

His words hang in the air as I think about the days to come. Paloma and I went from friends to lovers to strangers. I'm not sure if we could ever get back to friends.

And I don't know if I'm okay with that reality.

Paloma

CHAPTER FIVE

LACEY HELPS me haul my suitcase and guitar case in the taxi in front of our house, wiping her forehead even though she barely broke a sweat.

Her long, blonde hair sways in the cold wind as she turns to me with a bright smile.

"You're going to write the best damn songs you've ever written, and Graham will be so fucking regretful for what he did to you."

I give her a look and shake my head, laughing. "Hilarious, Lacey. You know I don't want this just as much as he doesn't. I don't even want to be in a writing studio alone with him, and now it's going to be a hotel room? Talk about suffocation with his ego."

Lacey pulls her arms across her chest as another gust of wind encases us. The taxi driver honks his horn and waves to me from the driver's seat. I give him an apologetic smile.

"You're going to do just fine and will be back within a few days! What could go wrong? I could even sneak in at night and we can have a sleepover! I'll bring popcorn and Valentina sauce."

My mouth waters at the thought of our favorite snack. "You don't have to sneak in," I giggle. "It's not a restricted hotel. I don't think anyone is going to be checking in on us except for Montrose calling or texting. They just expect the demos to be recorded by the end of this trip. They'll get our shitty hotel room acoustics on a voice memo."

"Well, then, seems like you're all good to go. I'll come over tomorrow night?"

I nod, reaching for a hug as she does the same. Her taller frame encases mine. When we pull apart, her bright blue eyes are sparkling with tears. This instantly brings tears to my own eyes.

"Don't you dare, Lace," I say sternly. Lacey and I have been best friends since high school back in North Carolina. She was quick to hop on the dream bandwagon with me when I was twenty-one, ready to pack everything I own and head to Music City. We've lived in the Edgehill neighborhood in a cutesy cottage since, and never plan to leave unless one of us gets married—that was our promise the moment we realized we're basically soul sisters and could thrive here if we just had each other.

She's the yin to my yang. The blondie to my brunette. The friend who pushes me to be the best person I can be in an industry that tries to pull you apart at the seams with its sharp-edged teeth. Lacey might be a manager at the wine bar around the corner, but she has supported me in all my whimsical dreams.

"Write the damn songs and I'll see you in a bit, okay?" she whispers before she hugs herself again through another gust of wind. The December weather is normally cold, but it seems to be getting chillier recently. Snow doesn't come to Nashville until late January or February, so it's odd that it's getting like this.

"Alright, I'll text you when I get to my room," I promise before hitching my purse strap higher up on my shoulder and heading to the taxi. It's almost seven in the morning, so traffic shouldn't be too bad to get to the hotel. Montrose texted me the address last night.

"Write your heart out, Songbird," Lacey replies with the nickname she gave me the moment I whipped out a guitar years ago and played one of my favorite lullabies. She's called me that ever since.

I give her a wave before hopping in the taxi, and the driver huffs out a loud breath. I keep from rolling my eyes before thanking him for waiting, and he zips out of the neighborhood.

THE TAXI STOPS in front of the hotel that's close to the airport. *Huh*, that's odd, they chose one so close to where Graham and I live. We could've easily commuted ourselves this week.

Montrose is waiting in front of the entrance near the valet stand. He's waving to me, and I hop out of the taxi, thanking the driver for taking my suitcase out of the trunk. He gives me a glare before getting back in his car and driving off.

"There's been a change of plans," Montrose calls out as I roll my suitcase and guitar case closer to him. I raise a brow and that's when I see Graham coming out of the lobby entrance doors. I try to make my heart stop pattering so fast at the sight of him.

He's wearing a green sweater that hugs all the right muscles and then some straight leg jeans and his staple faded cowboy boots. His hands are full of his guitar case and duffel, mirroring my own state.

"What's going on?" I ask, finally reaching them both, and Montrose's lips twist into a frown. Graham is silent, looking anywhere but at me.

"Colbie would rather you guys spend time truly secluded in a place no one can bother you to make this record."

"EP," Graham and I say almost simultaneously, and we glance at each other for a moment. Heat flushes my neck and cheeks, but neither men notice.

"We're at the hotel, isn't that secluded enough?" I counter, nodding to the entrance.

Montrose shifts his weight from one foot to another and crosses his arms over his chest. "She rented out a cabin in Frost-pine Hollow and has her private jet waiting to bring you there pronto."

My eyes practically bug out of my head, and Graham finally speaks up. "You're joking, right? Does she think we're incapable of making a few songs for her? We agreed to do this, why does it have to be this complicated?"

I can tell he wants to spit a few more words at Montrose, but our manager just holds up his hand and presses his lips together in a tight line.

"That's what I tried to tell her, but she's already got the head of the label on board and they agreed. Loren is *ecstatic* about it. They already cancelled the hotel reservations before you both arrived." We hear a honk from a tinted SUV pulling up to the hotel's driveway. "And that's our ride to her private jet. Let's not keep Colbie Brooks waiting, right?"

Graham sighs and rolls his shoulders back, a tell that he's annoyed but won't speak his mind to save face. His eyes also show worry.

He hates flying; he'd rather drive cross-country from Nash-ville to LA if he had to, anytime we had writing sessions with artists in the past. He never really told me where this fear came from, but I can see it's very evident in the way he's looking right now.

"Come on, hurry up," Montrose waves at us as he turns and heads to the SUV. I follow quickly, nudging Graham's elbow as I pass, and it seems to do the trick, getting him out of the trance he's in. He follows closely behind me, his guitar case hitting the back of my thigh for a moment before we reach the SUV.

Once we're settled inside, the car ride is quiet. Montrose is giving us time to think over the new reality before us, and I silently thank him for it. Being our manager has not only made him aware of the type of contracts we deserve, but he also understands when we need our space.

Because I'm not so sure how I'll survive the next few days alone with Graham Westin in a cabin in the middle of the mountains.

This wasn't the Christmas miracle I was begging Ferris for.

Graham

CHAPTER SIX

I HATE FLYING WITH A PASSION. Being a songwriter and having to travel to different states to meet up with artists wasn't something I thought of when I got signed on to Indigo Roots.

The smaller the plane, the worse my anxiety gets. Although the trip from Nashville to the tiny airport strip in Frostpine Hollow was an hour in the private jet, it felt like an eternity. No amount of deep breathing, listening to ocean sounds in my noise-cancellation headphones, and wearing a sleeping mask could keep me from wanting to steal a parachute and say *adios* to Paloma and Montrose.

It didn't help that anytime I lifted the eye mask a smidge to peek out, I'd make eye contact with the woman who still made my stomach flutter and heart race.

She's absolutely exhausting my emotional bandwidth I'm so desperately trying to run from.

The landing of the jet is smoother than I hoped, and I almost kiss the damn ground the moment we deplane and set foot in the mountain town. Montrose points us to the rental car the label so graciously got us, but to our surprise, it wasn't the SUV that would survive in any weather. We got the last pick of the litter and stood in front of a damn tiny box car that could barely fit our suitcases, let alone our guitars.

I groan, taking the keys from Montrose as he starts to step back onto the staircase leading into the jet. My hand clenches the keys tightly, letting the pain of the metal piercing my skin distract me from wanting to scream.

"We'll be fine!" Paloma's chirpy voice breaks my thoughts and I finally let out a snort. I turn to yell at Montrose, but he's got the smart idea to hop back in the jet and wave to us from one of the windows.

I look down at Paloma, who is still trying to get the guitar cases to fit in the backseat, when she turns to glance at me. Her cheeks turn red.

"I don't think I'll fit in this damn box," I retort, shuffling closer to the vehicle. It's bright blue and a sight for sore eyes. It's ugly and seems to be fitting for the hell of a show this trip is giving us already.

Paloma waves her fingers, dismissing my negativity. Like a fairy throwing pixie dust in the air, making all the problems disappear. If only it was that easy, we wouldn't be in this predicament.

"You don't have to be happy about this, Sugarplum." The words are out of my mouth before I can catch myself. Sugarplum? Where the hell did that come from?

Her brows cinch together before she smiles. "I'm not happy, but this is what we have to deal with. Don't be such a grump…" She pauses and thinks for a moment, standing straight and looking up at me. I roll my shoulders back and hold my breath for her insult that's sure to be coming. "Don't be a grouch, Graham. It's not a good look."

I chuckle, a smirk plastering on my face. This seems to make her a bit more on edge and it's making me want to keep pushing her sugarplum buttons. "Is that so? Is this how we're going to be this whole trip? Don't think any songs will be written."

"I'm fine with that, Frostbite."

Frostbite? Really? Can she be any more creative than that? A laugh escapes me and I step back, stumbling a bit for show and allowing the laughter to bubble out of my chest. She places her hands on her hips and huffs out a breath. "See! You're such an inane…" She stomps her cute boots into the concrete tarmac.

"Finish that thought, Sugarplum, please. I can wait all day, it's not like we have anywhere to be." I walk around her and head to the driver's side, leaning up against the car frame. She gets on her tiptoes and shoots daggers with her eyes from over the car's roof.

"I hope I get Frostbite in my eyes so I never have to see you again," she mutters.

"Oh, so scary, sweetheart," I immediately pipe back. If she was an animated cartoon, I know she'd have steam coming out of her ears and a red face, ready to blow.

"Whatever, I'm going to call Montrose at the cabin and tell him I can't do this. This was clearly a mistake."

"Well, that's the spirit. We'll make this cabin trip a solo vacation. I'll stick to one side of the cabin and you'll stick to yours. I'll even stop at a gas station to find tape to mark off the halfway points. I get the kitchen, though."

She stomps her foot again and opens the passenger door, getting inside. I smile, knowing I won this little face-off.

Graham: 1

Paloma: 0

I open the door and slide in, as best as I can with my 6'1 frame. The car isn't as bad as I thought, but it's not the most comfortable. Paloma, on the other hand, seems to have all the room in the world to swing her legs this way and that to get comfortable.

"You're so sweet to me, Sugarplum," I almost whisper, putting the keys into the ignition and turning the car on.

"Just drive, Graham," Paloma replies softly, and I glance at her for a moment, watching her features fall. The feeling of guilt creeps in, and I want to take back the last couple of minutes of shit talking we just did.

The drive to the mountain cabin is forty minutes, so I turn on the radio and tune in to the country station. A new song is playing that I've heard a few times this week. It's catchy and uplifts my spirits a bit.

She turns to look out the window and doesn't say another word. I don't either.

"YOU'VE GOT to be kidding me."

"What?" Paloma's voice is groggy from her catnap and she lifts her head from the headrest to look up at what I'm seeing. What *we're* seeing now.

The cabin is *huge*. Like it can fit a family huge. It's not fit for two people who just need a place to write songs.

"You must've put in the wrong address," she blankly states. My neck almost cracks at how fast I whip it to look at her.

"This is the correct address, honey bun," I quip.

"Can you quit calling me those names? God, you weren't this sickly sweet when we were together with the pet names," she starts, leaning her neck back to stretch from her nap.

I turn off the car and raise a hand in truce. "Sorry, won't happen again…for the next hour. This is my way of processing our situation."

She laughs, a real Paloma laugh, and I can't help but smile at that. I quickly wipe it off my face before she can notice. "Right, if calling me an obscene amount of names gets you through this trip, then go ahead. I'll allow it."

"Thanks, princess."

"I hope your writing is better than this," she throws back and I shake my head, unbuckling my seatbelt and getting out of the car. She follows suit, stretching her arms up in the air, and I twist my back and stretch my own legs for a moment. Damn small car.

"You know my writing, darling."

"Unfortunately," she says, but then she pauses and heads to the backseat door and opens it, taking out our guitar cases. "I didn't mean that."

My hands are quick to grab my case from her, but she side-steps me and nods toward the trunk. "You can punch me with your words all you want, Paloma. I deserve it."

While I open the trunk and pull out our suitcases, she's quiet. I don't dare to look at her to see her expression. The way we ended was completely on me and there are some things she'll never truly know about that time. Some of those *words* that explain some of my faults are sitting in that case in her pretty little hands. Just like she once held my heart.

Montrose texted us the cabin key code, so I'm quick to put it in, the lock whirring, and before we know it, we're inside. Paloma lets out a loud breath and I almost do the same. It's beautiful here.

It's a traditional-style cabin with log walls and wooden beams, but has updated appliances and floor-to-ceiling windows all over. A beautiful and breathtaking fireplace with a brick-style mantle at the far end of the living room. It's like an escape to the mountains with a modern twist for those who don't want to exactly camp in a tent. The porch wraps around the whole place and the kitchen is something I've never seen before.

We take our time looking everywhere and find a hot tub in the back that overlooks the beautiful view of the Smoky Mountains. Frostpine Hollow has always been known for the best views of the mountains during all four seasons. Although it's much colder out here than in Nashville, I don't think we'll see much snow.

There's a master suite bedroom on the first floor, and another on the second floor, adjoined to another living room with floor-to-ceiling windows and an office with a bunk bed. The basement is equipped with a built-in bar, an entertainment area with a pool table and a ping pong table, a sauna, and a theater room. The main floor has state-of-the-art kitchen appliances, a huge living room with the coziest cloud couches and chairs, and a piano in the corner.

"This place is going to inspire me so much," Paloma finally speaks up as we gather back at the front foyer, as she gathers her suitcase from the ground where I left it.

"Which bedroom do you want?" I ask, gathering my own suitcase and guitar. She looks around the area once more before nodding toward the ceiling.

"I'll take the upstairs room. Then, in case a burglar comes, they'll kidnap you first."

I laugh at that and raise a brow. "Kidnap me? Really? Think I can't defend my own?"

A small smile breaks from her lips that I remember once being so soft. I wonder if they still are… "You can, Graham. Just wanted to see your reaction." She starts to head toward the stairs before looking back at me. "Want to meet in thirty to head to town for groceries and dinner? I could eat a big plate of pancakes and bacon right about now."

Breakfast for dinner. A Paloma staple.

"Sure, sounds good," I reply, watching her climb the stairs as best as she can with her suitcase. She left her guitar down here, but I don't bother letting her know. Knowing Paloma, she wants to keep it in the place we'll use it most, like the living room.

I head to the master suite to the far right of the cabin, throw the suitcase on the bed, and unzip it, gathering what I need to refresh before our trip to town.

That's when I see a piece of paper folded on top of some of my clothes. *That wasn't there before*.

Damn Stetson. He definitely snuck it in there when I wasn't looking last night. I pick it up and unfold it, reading the scribbled note.

Now that you're alone with her, maybe show her that song you wrote that night. Yeah, that one.

My jaw clenches and I toss the paper aside, letting it fall to the ground.

I'd rather eat a bowl full of screws than do that, Stetson. *No way.*

Paloma

CHAPTER SEVEN

THE DINER we're at is cute and definitely a small-town staple that locals know of. We're at the edge of town, so a bit from the downtown area where tourists flood the streets in Frostpine Hollow. It's even got a cute name: *Smoky Biscuits*. There's a cute family of bears on the logo on top of the restaurant, sitting at a log table with plates full of diner food.

I've only ever been to this town as a kid during the summers for the theme park they have nearby, so this diner is new to me and I'm a bit excited. I've yet to stay in a cabin with the view we have this week. It feels like I've crossed something off my bucket list, but being reminded I'm here with someone I thought I'd never have to see again makes me want to keep it un-crossed.

Graham is chowing down on his plate of steak and eggs while I'm cutting up my pancakes into smaller pieces. I've drenched the cakes with so much syrup I could feed all of Santa's elves if I needed to this holiday season.

"That good?" I laugh in between bites while he takes another big one before grabbing his chocolate milk and gulping it like he hasn't had a sip of water in days. He's such a child. I hate to admit it, but the image in front of me is cute.

He nods before grabbing a napkin and wiping his mouth. "This is the best breakfast for dinner I've had in a while."

"Guess you missed me, huh?" I say without thinking and it grows silent around the table we're at. His piercing green eyes stay on me and it makes my face heat up.

"You could say that, Sugarplum."

I roll my eyes and groan before stabbing my fork into another piece of pancake, shoving it in my mouth. The syrupy goodness fills my soul and warms my body with holiday cheer. "Stop calling me that!"

"Why?" He grins, licking his lips. "Hate the way it makes *you* miss *me*?"

I take a bite and swallow. "What makes you think I miss you?"

His eyes narrow. "Your cheeks are bright red. I know your tells, Paloma."

Hearing him say my name instead of one of those stupid nicknames makes my heart thump a little harder in my chest. *What the hell?*

I reach for my orange juice and take a long sip. "It's cold outside, that's the reason."

He checks his watch quickly and shrugs. "I mean, it's twenty degrees colder than Nashville, so that might be the case, but I think my statement rings true."

"You're an awfully unreliable narrator, then," I retort and go back to eating my pancakes. He's finally quiet for a moment as we finish eating our dinner.

My eyes can't help but gravitate toward him and I mentally trace the lines of his nose, jawline, and anything else my mind can do. I don't know why I'm letting myself do this, but it's nice being in this diner hundreds of miles away from home. With Graham.

It feels like the ice around me is slowly melting and being chipped away the longer we're alone. Far from the pressures of Music City and the demands of our label. Far from the wandering eyes of friends wanting to know why we broke up and why we can't get back together.

Far from the wall I've put up in my heart that has kept me from truly songwriting all these years...

My fingers itch for my journal and guitar at this moment, causing a flutter of butterflies to escape in my stomach. Graham doesn't seem to notice the change in temperature I'm feeling—rosy cheeks and all.

He pays for the check, which I offer to split, but he doesn't bat an eye as he slaps his card on the table, and we get up to head back to the parking lot. He's got his hands jammed in the front pockets of his jeans and mine are in my coat. I hate this weather and wish I had packed more winter clothes. If I could be dressed in a heated blanket from head to toe, I would.

"That was yummy," I state, kicking my shoe at the ground awkwardly. He chuckles and nods, leaning against the driver's side of the small car. He looks so funny next to it, like a giant next to a marshmallow.

"It was, I wish I wasn't here for work, or else I'd feel like I can enjoy it more."

His words take me by surprise, and I raise a brow. "Really?"

He nods. "Feel like I have to be acting a certain way while on the clock, you know?"

"We don't clock in," I remind him, smiling.

He finally lets out a loud exhale and smiles. "You know what I mean, Sugar—" He stops mid-nickname, and I can see his eyes twinkle in the dark sky. The sun is long gone by now and the wind has picked up a bit, causing me to shiver in my winter boots.

"Yeah, I know," I whisper before wrapping my arms around myself. He unlocks the car.

"Get in, I forgot how much you hate the cold. What a perfect location then, huh?"

I roll my eyes and happily oblige as he cranks up the heat once we're both settled inside. The drive to the nearby market isn't long, and we decide to divide and conquer so we don't waste too much time and can get back to the cabin in one piece.

By the time we make it back to the cabin, put the groceries away, and change into more comfortable clothes, it's almost 9 p.m.

Graham is in the living room with his guitar, strumming a few chords. I grab my case and take my guitar out, careful not to mess with any of the song sheets I have in there. I grab the capo, too, in case I need it. I decide on the comfy seat next to the couch and nestle myself and Lucie, my guitar, onto it.

"Got any ideas for the EP?" I ask, quickly tuning my guitar from the change of weather. The windows are already frosting from the colder weather, and the heater is on, buzzing in the background. Just enough where we're not shivering but also not too much where we're sweating.

I'm wearing one of my favorite winter cardigans, a deep blue with snowflake buttons, along with some leggings and chunky socks. Graham is wearing a loose-fitting shirt with a random band etched on it and gray sweatpants. His disheveled hair fits perfectly with his relaxed fit, and I can't help but blush at the sight.

"Not a clue. I was thinking anything that rhymes with Rudolph or Santa Claus."

"Sandy paws," I joke. He chuckles before stopping his strumming and grabbing his journal from the coffee table in front of us. He flips to a new page.

"We need five songs and obviously one needs to be a love song," he mentions. Montrose gave us a bit of information on what Colbie wants from us while we were on the plane. At least five songs, one romantic duet, and a ton of Christmas cheer sprinkled in.

"Obviously," I repeat, the room suddenly gets quiet. We both glance at each other for a second before we return our gaze to our guitars and his journal. It's not ideal for me to be sitting so far away from him; I should really be directly across or next to him, but I'm not ready for that close proximity right now.

"We could make a cute jingle about Christmas and all that fun stuff," he says, writing the idea down in the journal. I nod, but begin to nibble on my bottom lip.

"We can, but is that what she wants? I think we need to write with a theme."

"Like all lovey dovey?" He raises a brow.

I shake my head. "No, but that would be the love song. It could be a theme of romance. Maybe some about yearning, loss, or even heartbreak. Then the lovey dovey one. We don't necessarily have to bring in Christmas cheer in every song. We can settle for one, I think."

"I like that," he says with a nod. He puts down the journal and strums a bit more and hums, eyes closing. His brows pinch together as he thinks hard. It's an expression I've come to understand so well over the course of not only working with Graham but dating him. He gets so immersed in his songwriting that it's clear this is his passion. There's no faking it. The results of his words are spread all over the radio and in his journal…and in my heart. The latter is something I've closed myself off from thinking about ever since the breakup.

I can tell that he's cooking up a melody in his head, so I don't disturb him. That's what I miss the most about writing with Graham—we work so well together once we start. He finds the melody and then I make the lyrics. He perfects the words until we both feel that 'aha' moment. He's a great lyricist as well, don't get me wrong, but this process has worked the best when we're in the same room.

I've listened to all his songs that he's shown me in and out of the studio, as well as whatever he writes for musicians that end up on the radio. I've never once not tuned into his songs. I'm proud of him, no matter where we ended things.

Since he's got it going, I put my guitar down and grab my own journal quickly from my case and return to my seat, tapping my pink glittery pen against my lips.

Santa might be coming down his way

But I know I've got no present on his sleigh

"That's stupid." I laugh. Graham stops strumming and I bite the inside of my cheek and look up from the journal. He raises a brow.

"Oh yeah? Tell me what you got, Sugarplum."

I repeat the first half of the verse to him, and he smiles. "What?" I laugh.

"It's actually not bad. I like it. Keep writing. Or singing, whichever you want to do."

This makes me smile from cheek to cheek and nod. My chest begins to warm and it's like I'm back to being myself in this room with my guitar and journal. The words are flowing out of me like never before. Montrose would be so proud to know I'm actually writing again and not relying on old works to throw at the label.

The bells are ringing loud and clear tonight

There's no reason for me to stay awake through the night

I shake my head, crossing out a few words and making it flow better.

No reason to stay awake through the night

I stare at the words and twist my lips together. Does that sound like it flows? Graham clears his throat, and I look up, catching his expectant eyes. I repeat the next part of the verse to him.

"I like it," he confirms.

"It doesn't sound too cliche? I don't know why I'm sticking to an A-A-B-B rhyme scheme."

"I mean, we always chop up and refine our lyrics when we're ready, but I do like what we have so far. I mean it."

My heart flutters at those words. It feels like nothing's changed, being in this cabin with Graham. Yet, everything has changed. There's no denying that the past is finding its way back into the cracks of the foundation of this cabin, trying to get ahold of me—of us.

"I'll keep writing, you keep playing for the next verse, then we can move on to the chorus."

Graham nods at my directions and continues to strum while I think and write. The wind outside picks up, hitting the window pane and causing me to jump a bit. The forecast didn't call for snow up in the mountains where we are, but you never know with the unpredictable Tennessee weather, especially in Frost-pine Hollow.

It makes me think about the past few winters I've had in Nashville. The way snow tends to come late January and only lasts a week. It's different up in the mountains, but I've yet to experience it. It's pretty, but not something I really like. It's too cold, too unpredictable, and things just seem to go wrong when it's added into the mix.

I look at Graham a bit more while I think about the snow and cold and he locks eyes with me for a moment before giving me the faintest smile. The frosty emotions he's been giving me in Nashville seem to be thawing a bit, and I like seeing him be vulnerable again like this. The reason why I fell so hard for him years ago.

The lyrics flow out of me after I look back down and focus, the glittery pen working fast to keep up with my thoughts as it scribbles ink all over the page.

These cookies and milk are getting cold
Cause my heart ain't a heart of gold

Trying to get off the naughty list is useless
And now I'm nothing but reckless

I read out the lyrics to Graham and he nods before speaking up. "I like the first three lines, but maybe the last one can be refined. Better."

My eyes stare at the words until they no longer make sense. "What else rhymes with useless?"

"Reckless?" Graham smiles, scratching his chin for a moment, the guitar playing halting.

I shake my head and toss the journal on the coffee table with the pen. I get up and pace the room for a moment as I try to think of a better line. "Santa knows I'm on the naughty list…"

The guitar strums again and I turn to see Graham with his eyes closed. "And nice has never been my twist?"

"No, absolutely not." I laugh. "Why is this line so hard?" I groan and stomp back to the chair and plop down. Graham sighs from his place.

"Santa knows I'm on the naughty list, keeping you around my mind in a twist?"

My head picks up and I glance at the man before me. A damn lyricist. No wonder he got that huge deal and I didn't years ago.

"We can work with that, it's better than what I had," I confirm. I grab the journal and pen once more, chewing the inside of my cheek in deep concentration. The chorus needs to be catchy if this is the vibe we're going for.

Graham begins to bump up the beat with the chords and tempo of his strumming and my knees bounce to the rhythm. "I'm checking you once, twice, three times."

"Santa can't stop this wish of mine," I sing along.

"So come on over, it's something you already know." Graham strums the guitar a bit more intensely toward the end of the chorus.

"And get yourself under this mistletoe," I sing, finishing off the chorus.

"Under this mistletoe," we both sing.

It's silent for a moment as we let the guitar finish out, echoing the last chord around the living room. Graham and I both look at each other and smile. My heart flutters again at the magic we just made.

"I've missed this, Paloma," Graham finally says with a loud exhale and everything seems to stop.

"Me too."

Graham

CHAPTER EIGHT

I **HEAD** to the kitchen the next morning and start looking for the coffee maker in the millions of cabinets surrounding me. The landscape right outside the floor-to-ceiling windows is breathtaking, and I have a mission: make a good cup of Joe and go out there to enjoy it.

My phone buzzes as I find the damn coffee maker and pull it out onto the counter, along with my phone from my pajama pants pocket.

STETSON

How did the first night go with P?

ME

We wrote a song

STETSON

no way… thought you'd come back with maybe half a song and a laundry list of complaints.

ME

Might be this one song. Who knows.

STETSON

I'll check in again later to see the progress

ME

You don't have to 😌

STETSON

I know your icy heart is not letting you mend things with her

Damn Grinch

ME

Woah, don't go that far!

STETSON

Then prove me wrong

I sent my best friend another text of emojis before focusing on the coffee and pulling out all the things I'd need from our grocery trip last night. By the time the coffee is brewing, Paloma's steps are loud against the stairs, and she waltzes in. Her hair is unbrushed, frizzy at the top, and trickles down her shoulders like a waterfall. Her cheeks are rosy and she's decked out in blue snowflake pajamas and chunky red slippers with a white bow on top.

"Good morning, sleeping beauty," I sing as she grimaces and yawns before heading straight to the cabinet filled with mugs. I rush to reach above her head to grab one as well. She jumps a bit at the sudden movement from me, and I chuckle.

"I slept great, almost missed my alarm," she mumbles, heading for the coffee maker. My fingers wiggle toward her mug, and she obliges, handing it over. I pour us both a cup of coffee before setting them on the counter. We are quiet as we add sugar and creamer before I finally speak up.

"If you did, I would've woken you."

She smiles over the rim of her coffee mug. "Yeah? How so?"

I think for a moment. "Blasted your favorite Christmas songs. Frosty the Snowman."

"Please, no," she states before stepping away from the kitchen counter and heading to the living room. I follow her instinctively before remembering my plan to go out on the balcony.

"Care to join me outside?" I ask, pivoting toward the door.

She shakes her head and sits down, pulling a blanket over her lower half. She takes another sip of the hot coffee before locking eyes with me. "I'm going to write in my journal. Trying to keep up my routine even away from home."

I give her a curt nod before heading outside, closing the door behind me. I've got a sweater on and I'm glad I decided to throw it on over my baggy shirt. It's colder than yesterday and I swear I can see my breath every time I exhale. The seats are cushioned, thankfully, and I sit down, letting my body relax.

The mountains are in the distance and I focus on those, tracing the peaks with my eyes and letting my breathing even out with the fresh air. It feels like my lungs are working overtime due to the cold, but it makes my body feel better. As if the air is filtering everything inside me. All the bad.

Thoughts of last night come back to me and I let my mind relish in it. This cabin has been good to me and my writing. It's flowing more easily, and I feel like I'm able to lean into what I've been missing. I haven't really co-written with anyone else after Paloma. I'd help out other publishing houses with song sheets they'd send me, or I'd be called into a room to help fix a verse or two for another writer. But nothing like what Paloma and I have been doing in the past or what we did last night. It was nice and something I've missed.

The collaboration on songwriting feels so *us*. It makes me wonder if she's written with anyone else since we last parted. Does she write better songs now that I'm out of the picture?

Does she have a new writing partner that Colbie pulled her away from just to spend this week with me?

The thoughts start to circulate faster in my head, and I try to breathe deeply, allowing the mountain air to work its magic once more.

Ruminating on what Paloma and I once were isn't going to change what I've done to her.

I can only focus on now. And I will.

"ALRIGHT, my brain needs a break, and I don't think we're going to get another song written like this," Paloma cries out, tossing her journal on the floor beside her thigh.

We've resorted to writing on the ground after too many hours on the couch trying to fix up last night's song, then recording the memo for Colbie. We started another song before we started short-circuiting on the ideas, and Paloma got frustrated.

My brain was still in work mode and I didn't want to leave until we finished this last verse we were stuck on. Granted, we still needed a bridge, but that's beside the point.

"Come on, just one more hour," I ask her, starting to get annoyed that she wants to give up now. We're so close.

She looks at me and shakes her head, getting up. "If I have to think of another winter word or melody that sounds cheerful and Christmas-y, then I'm going to lose it."

"That's the whole reason we're here," I point out, sighing.

"Songs take time," Paloma counters. Now my head is starting to pound from hours of working and trying to deal with her.

"Yeah, you said that already."

She stomps toward the window and stares. "Colbie should've really thought this EP through. Who the hell writes a whole album in five days?"

"We have four more days and have already written one and started another, so maybe we'll break the world record," I say. That clearly isn't what she wants to hear and her head snaps toward me, eyes piercing through my soul.

"That's not even a song a day with our progress. You'd think they'd give us a full week. Seven days."

"I know how many days are in a week, Sugarplum."

"Yeah? Do you? Then go write the damn songs yourself!" Her voice cracks, and she turns swiftly, heading toward her journal to snatch it, then walks toward the stairs. I sigh and get up, my legs aching to be stretched, and I wince from the position they were stuck in for the last few hours.

"That doesn't even make sense. Don't be like that, P!" I almost scream.

"Like what?" She twists around to stare at me again, and I swear I can see steam coming out of her ears. The wind outside picks up and I glance at the window briefly, seeing the trees sway.

I shrug finally. "You're just confusing me. Let's finish this song and then have a break for the rest of the evening and night. I can make us pizza."

By the way her lips twist and turn, I can tell she's thinking of a million things to call me. I don't know what has gotten into her, but it's starting to affect my mood as well as make this pounding in my head get louder and harsher. Now I'm starting to feel agitated alongside her.

"I can't. We've been at this for hours. I need to rest before I have to finish this damn thing."

"Alright," I finally surrender. "I'll be here trying to finish it myself and I'll let you know how it goes when you're ready to come back downstairs."

She's quiet before nodding. She doesn't say anything—she's quick to run up the stairs and the slamming of her bedroom door echoes around the cabin. I sigh once more, running my hands over my face.

I whip out my phone and call Montrose. He picks up on the third ring. "How are my favorite writers?"

I groan. "Not doing so well today."

His voice is cheery, but the moment he hears me, it changes to worry. "What's going on?"

"We're stuck on this second song and Paloma won't power through."

"How long have you guys been at it?"

I think of the time we started and start to count. "Six hours," I tell him.

Montrose lets out a noise before gasping. "That long and a song wasn't finished? What's going on?"

"I think we're broken," I confess.

This makes Montrose laugh and it doesn't make the situation better. Paloma is in her room doing God knows what, and I'm here trying to salvage this song. I feel the hopelessness set in, and the agitation grows.

"You're not broken. You've just hit a speed bump. Over-working your brain will do that to you creatives."

"But we need this done quickly," I remind him.

"I know," he says with a sigh. "I can see if Colbie can hold off a day or two. Can you send me the voice memos as soon as they're ready? That might help speed up the process on her end and allow you more time to write."

"Yeah, I guess that helps. I can get Paloma to send over the lyrics as well. We got the first song finalized and the voice memo done. But this second song…"

"Don't worry about it, Graham. I'll do what I can on my end, and you rest your brain and get back to it either later tonight or tomorrow."

"Thanks, Monty," I reply, feeling a bit better after the call.

He ends the call with a goodbye, and I contemplate going upstairs to tell Paloma. Or even texting it to her.

But I hold off. I want to give her space and time to cool down. To rest her mind before we're back at it. We have this second song to finish and edit before moving on to the other three. Thinking about the romantic duet we'll have to eventually write makes my skin crawl.

Writing with Paloma this go around is different from the objective of a Christmas EP. I think we're both holding off on that damn duet until the last possible moment because it's not going to end well. Feelings are going to be hurt once we start.

Writing vulnerable love songs is our strongest suit, but right now it's the worst thing in the world. It's going to open a can of worms that we've tried to keep shut for so long.

My feelings can be handled and I'll just push them down, but I'm afraid Paloma isn't going to be the same.

Because once she finds out the truth that will inevitably seep out of me while we write that damn duet, she is going to want to run for the mountains and never look back.

And I'm not ready for that to happen when we finally find a way to come back together despite the circumstances.

Paloma

CHAPTER NINE

"WHERE ARE WE GOING?" I ask Graham, peeking out the car window, but seeing barely anything. The weather has definitely picked up and the windows keep frosting no matter how much he tries to adjust the heater.

"You'll see," is all that Graham replies with as he continues down the path of road that is starting to look like an entrance to my death. The sun is long gone and I'm not even sure if he knows where he's going.

He's going to probably drop me off in the middle of the mountains with how much of a bitch I've been today. It wasn't until I took a nap, showered, and ate something that I felt much better after our grueling writing session. Six hours and nothing to count for it but two verses. How the hell did we write a song the first night?

Graham starts to slow the car, and that's when I see some buildings finally take shape in the distance, and the street lights flicker. We're back in the downtown square, where there seem to be a lot of people out despite the cold weather that has come on quickly. I swear I saw a snowflake earlier.

Couples in comfy outfits, some dressed up for a fancy dinner, and then the casual tourists waltzing about the square, ready for their next adventure. Some kids are running and screaming here and there.

"Please tell me we're getting cheese curds," I pipe up, looking at Graham. He smiles and shakes his head as he turns the wheel, and the car swerves into another street.

"I'm sure they have it there, but I was thinking a dive bar for some music and darts."

"And pool?" I ask, thinking back to some nights when our creative juices were drained and we needed to get out of the studio and head to the nearby dive bar. We spent so many nights there that the bartender knew us by name and we practically had a pool table and dart board assigned to us.

"And pool if they have a table. This seems to be a really small town, so who knows."

He finds a free spot on the street and backs into it before turning off the car. We get out and the brisk wind hits us like a train. I instantly shiver and pull my arms around my chest, trying to warm up before I get sick. Nothing worse than trying to sing with a sore throat or think of lyrics with a pounding headache.

Graham gets to the sidewalk where I'm at and pulls me by the shoulders, his body heat instantaneously warming me up. It's not a romantic gesture, more like a friend pulling you in, but my cheeks warm at the movement.

"Thanks," I mumble as he leads us toward whatever dive bar he's navigated us toward.

Stores around us are starting to close for the night, but restaurants and bars are bright with lights and people inside. I love people-watching through windows, and this is like Christmas: being able to walk through this small downtown area and look inside places to see different lives milling about. So many stories that I don't know of, just existing. So close, but out of reach.

"Here we are," he says loudly before steering our bodies to the front doors of a dive bar that looks like it was plucked right out of the outskirts of Nashville. Like the ones we would try to find on weekends when we didn't want to stay in the city.

Shiney on the Frost

"Funny," I mention, nodding to the name, and Graham laughs.

"A moonshine play on 'on the rocks', I like it," he responds.

"I wonder how many people actually order liquor or moonshine over beer here, though."

"It's a funny name, Sugarplum, don't think too much on it."

I roll my eyes, and he squeezes my shoulder before opening the door for me. But the moment we step inside, he keeps his distance, as if he doesn't want anyone to know that we're together or holding onto each other in the cold like we just were moments before.

"Welcome to *Shiney on the Frost,* where you can try some moonshine or whatever your soul desires," the bartender calls out to us. The place isn't too busy, but it looks like there's enough people, like locals coming for their nightcap. Christmas music filters throughout, and there are decorations that I hope will keep Graham in a better mood. I listen closely and realize the jukebox is playing *All I Want For Christmas Is You.* Cliche.

I catch the eyes of some of the patrons as we walk further into the bar and head to the bar. The bartender is an older gentleman with a white beard and friendly blue eyes. His back is a little hunched as he walks toward us, and I instantly want to know his story. Did he grow up in Frostpine Hollow? Is he married? Widowed? Have any rivals in this town?

Graham nudges me and that's when I realize they've been talking and asked me a question.

"What?" I ask, staring at them. Graham seems to be on edge and his lips twist for a moment before the bartender nods at me.

"What would you like, sweetheart?"

I think for a moment. "Just a Miller Lite if you have."

"Bottle or can? Not that fancy of a place to have it on draft."

He starts to walk toward a fridge behind him and waits for my answer. I tell him a bottle is fine and he pulls one out, grabbing a bottle opener from the counter and popping it off for me before sliding it on the bar counter. I grab it, the cold bottle making me shiver already. The temperature here is nice, but I could be a bit warmer. This cold beer probably won't help.

Graham asks for a seltzer, and I look at him like he just asked for a steak and a glass of wine. He eyes me for a moment as the old man gets him his drink. It's watermelon flavored and I can't keep the giggle from bubbling out of me.

"Looks like he wanted something fruity tonight," the bartender speaks up, giving him a smile before moving on to clean the counters and help another patron.

"Don't look at me like that," Graham states, taking a sip of the seltzer.

"Like what? I'm honestly surprised at your drink choice."

He shrugs. "Seltzers don't really affect me. I'd need like ten of these to really feel anything."

"And you don't want that?" I ask, taking a sip of my beer. It's not as tasty as a cocktail, but it'll do. I don't like seltzers because they're so carbonated.

"Not if I'm driving," he notes, and that's when I want to bite my tongue, or take back my mockery. He's being smart about driving, and here I am making fun of him for not drinking something more potent. *An ass move, Paloma.*

"Right," I say before turning around and surveying the bar. There are people sitting at tables, booths, and at the bar as well. Looks like an array of ages in here, so I don't feel like we stick out like a sore thumb.

"Why don't we go to that pool table over there?" Graham says, pushing himself off the bar counter and heading toward the table in the corner. It's the only one in the bar and I'm surprised it's not being used. But it looks like there's a small stage with a computer and table being set up. Probably trivia or bingo. There are also some TVs playing reruns of games from all kinds of sports: golf, basketball, and football.

I don't say anything and follow his lead. His tall figure looms over me and my eyes are stuck on his broad shoulders. His sweater is thicker than yesterday and it looks cozy. It's blue with some evergreen trees and then guitars dancing around the top. It's a winter sweater that I bet would look like a dress on me.

The image of that alone makes my body warm, and I take another pull of the beer before allowing it to take up residence in my mind. He grabs the rack and starts filling it with the billiard balls, and I grab two cues from the wall to our right.

Once the table is set up, he takes a cue from me and hits the cue ball into the formation, and the balls shoot everywhere. He's always been better at this than me.

"Solids," he calls out, clicking his tongue. I nod, seeing him make one more shot before missing the next one. I grab the cue ball from the bottom of the table and place it where I need to in order to hit the maroon stripes I've been eyeing. He lined it up perfectly for me as it sits right near a pocket. I call it out, hit the cue ball, and it straight shots into the maroon-striped ball, which goes into the pocket. I can't help but cheer and laugh.

"Nice," Graham calls out as I make two more striped balls into pockets before missing one. We continue this for a few more minutes, making sure to take pulls of our drinks before resuming. By the time we finish the first game, I'm ordering another beer from the old man bartender, who finally let me know his name, Barney. I get a water for Graham as well.

He's being more and more quiet the more the night goes on, and I can tell that he's stuck in his head. I want to tell him that he could get another drink if he wants to just relax for the night, but I know he won't allow himself to.

"Here," I say, giving him his water after he sets up the next game. He thanks me, taking the cup and taking a sip before nodding to the table.

"Winner starts first," he states. I gladly start the new game, and the music picks up around us as the patrons start hollering, and we both look at the commotion. Barney is coming up to the small stage and taking the mic.

"You know what time it is," he calls out to everyone.

"Karaoke!" a few older women scream from a table and then laughter booms from other people.

Graham shakes his head and smiles. "No way."

"You should sing *You're a Mean One, Mr. Grinch.*"

"Ha-Ha." He pouts and crosses his arms over his chest like a little kid. It looks cute on him, but then his eyes narrow and I know he's annoyed.

"Alright, fine, but I'm getting a water," I say, meeting Barney at the bar counter just as he's getting off the stage, where another worker is setting up the karaoke machine.

"Gonna sing for us?" he asks, nodding to the stage.

"Oh, no, I sing in the shower or in the comfort of my room," I tell him quickly. He raises his brow.

"Where are you guys from?"

"Nashville," I breathe out. The sudden spark in his eyes light up like a Christmas tree. And like the various Christmas decorations that look like they have been thrown up around the bar. The reindeer with Christmas lights around its antlers is staring me down from the top shelf of the bar above Barney.

"So you're a famous country star trying to escape your fans in a small town," he jokes, wiggling his brows.

"Not quite, but I've met many of them! Sadly, I won't be singing tonight, I'll just have another round and a water."

Barney nods before filling a cup of ice with water and then handing me another open beer. I thank him before I turn around, but that's when I catch Graham across the room, talking to a couple of guys, smiling wide. The way he laughs over something one of them says makes me a bit frustrated. Hurt.

He's so hot and cold, being kind to me in the cabin and on

the drive here, but then the meeting with Loren, and once we arrived at this bar, he flipped a switch? It feels like he's trying to portray a different lifestyle or personality in public. I just want him to be himself.

"You sure you don't wanna sing a song? Maybe a cute love song?" Barney calls behind me. That's when my hands clench around the beer bottle and water cup and I swiftly turn around.

"Sign me up, Barney. I'll play a song," I say quickly, telling him the song I want to play. There's an older woman singing her heart out on stage and Barney lets me know I'm two songs behind her so I head back to the pool table and place my drinks on the small table nearby.

Graham finally finishes his conversation and wanders back to me, grabbing his cue from the wall. "Another beer?"

"Yeah, why?" I ask, eyes narrowing. I can feel the annoyance start to bubble more.

He smirks. "Don't get too rowdy, Sugarplum."

"I'll be fine, Frosty," I bite back. The lady finishes singing and people clap before the next person comes on. But I don't tune in. I'm too focused on Graham and the way his ears get a bit red and his eyes get sharper. Like he's trying to intimidate me.

Well, it won't work. Not tonight.

"Are you still on medication?" His question pulls me out of our bubble and I'm suddenly back in this damn bar with him.

"What?" I'm so blindsided by the question that I can't think straight. His voice is softer now and he's leaning in when he repeats it. My mouth gapes open. "No, it's on a case-by-case basis now. I stopped taking it daily a year ago."

He nods, his lips pressing tightly together. He just hums.

"Why do you want to know?"

He shrugs. "Just want to make sure you're not drinking too much if you were still taking them consistently. You told me how alcohol affects you."

I roll my eyes and take a step back. He's being nice again in this brief moment, but I don't want to get sucked into that again. *Tricked* by him again. But it is nice that he remembered that important part about me.

"I'm fine, Graham. Trust me," I retort, and before I know it, the karaoke MC is calling out my name for me to get up on stage. Graham's eyes widen and he looks at me.

"Really? You're singing?"

I nod and stare at him before responding. "Barney thought we'd sing a duet, but you know how that turned out last time."

The words visibly cut him like a knife, and something in me regrets it, but I have to go on stage. I flip my hair behind my shoulder and head to the stage, grabbing a mic.

The song *Hot and Cold* by Katy Perry starts, and suddenly singing my heart out in this random dive bar is just what I need.

Graham

CHAPTER TEN

CHARMING. Fitting.

Paloma picked a song like she's trying to get me mad. Or push a message through my obviously dense skull. Either of which isn't what I was expecting.

The words appear on the screen and she starts singing, taking the crowd away with her magical voice. There's no doubt that she's the best singer in this room, sorry, old lady before her.

The guys I was just talking to, who were finance bros from Kentucky, looking for a getaway this week, turn to me and give me various whoops and thumbs up. I told them we weren't together, but our conversations started with them asking if Paloma was single while she went up to the bar for another round.

It wasn't that it made me jealous, per se, but it made me a bit more protective despite trying my best to put on a good smile. When she came back, I couldn't hide the fact that they annoyed me with their questions about her. I no longer warranted the protectiveness I once had over her, but since we were in a small town where we knew no one, I still felt like I had to.

Paloma sings the last chorus, and without a doubt, I knew

this was coming. She points to me. Her face is starting to heat up, but I just raise my can to her and smirk.

Graham: 1

Paloma: 1

So be it.

By the time she finishes, the whole bar is clapping and hollering at her and asking for another song. She waves her hands and shakes her head, laughing before hopping down and heading back to me. The table full of finance bros voice words of satisfaction and she even gives a few of them high fives. This, for some fucking reason, makes me want to snatch their hands away from her.

My jaw ticks as my teeth clench, and it's hard to hide my annoyance when she gives me a smile and raises a brow. "So? Was that better than a love duet?"

"It was very *calculated*," I try.

"Had to get a message out there for the Frostbite in the room," she quips. I scoff before turning back to the pool table and putting things back where we found them. If I can't punch these finance bros, then I'm going to throw darts at the board, picturing their faces on it. Especially the one that's still eyeing Paloma at this moment. I shoot him a glare before wrapping my arm around Paloma's shoulder as she picks up her drinks and finishes her beer, as I guide us back to Barney for the darts and marker.

"Knew you were something special," Barney sing-songs to Paloma and she blushes under me. She looks up from beneath her lashes and her pupils get a big larger.

"I had to make this grump get it together and singing seems to be the only way." Her dig at me should hurt more than it does, but I'm too transfixed on these emotions that are coursing through me. Wanting to protect her, wanting to let her do her thing. God, I really *am* hot and cold.

Fuck.

"Another round?" Barney asks. I let him know we want to play darts at the back of the bar, but he cocks his head at me.

"You sing too, don't you?"

"Was it the guitars on my sweater?" I chuckle, looking down at the design.

Barney laughs. "No, just the way you hold yourself around her," he says, nodding toward Paloma. "Y'all might not be famous country singers, but I can tell singing is something you both do together."

"You got us," Paloma finally confesses, her shoulders sagging for a moment as she exhales. I rub her shoulder with my palm and she seems to straighten a bit at the movement.

"We just write silly songs for commercials," I lie, wanting to end this and throw some darts. I hear nuance noises and turn my head to see the finance bros getting rowdier as they slam back more drinks.

"Bet you guys wrote some amazing love songs. Duets even?"

"Those are under lock and key," Paloma teases, elbowing me as best as she can in my hold. I let out a huff and squeeze her a bit more, which breaks out a giggle from her. A giggle that vibrates against me and ripples through my body.

"Sing one for me, dear?" Barney asks, leaning over the bar counter, reaching out for her. She places her empty water cup down and grabs his hand. "Sing for me, so I can remember my dear beloved, Carol."

Barney and Carol. Such sweet names. His eyes turn to sorrow and I feel for the man. I can't imagine losing a partner and having to continue life without them. My parents are still alive and well, married for over thirty years. I can't imagine if one of them passed not just for myself, but how the other would cope. They love each other to death.

Paloma looks up at me again and she's got an expression I know too well. The one where she wants to do something to benefit a person she truly cares about. We might've just met Barney tonight, but he's become a great soul to encounter. I think the least we could do is give him a song on stage. Three minutes and then we'll be done and can leave.

"Sure, we can do it," I finally tell him and Paloma. She smiles widely and steps a bit away from me so my arm drops from her shoulders, and she claps with one hand, still holding the beer.

"I know the perfect song!" She makes a beeline for the karaoke machine and tells the guy what song to play next. I raise my brows and smile at Barney.

"You guys have a story, I hope I get to hear about it one day," is all he tells me before the music starts and I have to dash on stage. Paloma hands me a mic, and the patrons clap and cheer for her since she came back for another song.

"I'm Paloma and this is Graham, and we'll be singing the lovely *I'll Be Home For Christmas* in honor of your very own Barney!" Her voice is angelic and flows through the bar like a flurry of snow, enveloping everyone. Barney claps and waves at us as we begin the song. This moment briefly brings me back to being at Sparrow's and doing this with Paloma.

She starts us off and closes her eyes, putting her best voice out there. I know she wants it to be perfect for Barney. When we first started working together years ago, she never thought she could sing well. I beg to differ with how the bar patrons are reacting to her voice—especially Barney.

By the time my part comes, I clear my throat and do my best as well. I glance at Paloma as I sing the verse, the older women hollering at me and the table of finance bros pumping their fists in the air. *So I guess I won't be picturing them on the dart board.*

We come together for the chorus again and our voices flow like honey dripping off a spoon. Steady, strong, and sweet. Complementing each other's vocals so well that I almost get a knot in my throat from how much I've missed this. The stage was never my dream, I've always wanted to be a songwriter and do my own thing with singing on the side, but being up here with Paloma makes me wonder what we could've done if I wasn't a selfish ass.

I push that thought and mountain of regret down as we finish the song and the bar erupts in applause and whoops and hollering. It's like we've got our own little concert going on with how lively everyone became with this song. Barney wipes tears from his eyes in the back, and Paloma jumps up and down before I face her, then pulls me in for a hug, wrapping her arms around my neck. Her perfume floods me and her hair suffocates my face, but I don't care.

I squeeze her back tightly and then we let go. We look at each other for a moment, and I tune out the bar and what's around us. I just see her.

"That was—" she says breathlessly.

"I know," I finish, turning to the crowd and doing a small bow. Barney claps loudly again, and the rest of the bar asks for an encore, but we encourage others to come up and continue singing. We make our way back to the bar where Barney's standing proudly.

"That was something else. I *felt* it," Barney exclaims. Paloma claps her hands and is giddy while I lean over to shake his hand. Barney is smiling from cheek to cheek, and I can't help but mirror him.

"I can't imagine we did that," Paloma says a bit loudly and her eyes are sparkling like no other.

"Me neither," I almost whisper.

"Remember what I said, sweetheart," Barney tells Paloma with a wink. She nods and looks at me once more. Once again, I feel pulled into her bubble. Her universe. I'm no longer at Barney's bar and I'm orbiting Paloma like a planet following its course around the sun.

I'm simply a man, and she's the sun and more.

"You'll hear it, if Frosty can't help it," she teases and her words bring me back to Earth. I raise a brow and look between the two.

"What do you mean?"

Barney laughs. "There's more to you two, I just know it. I'd like to hear about it one day."

"He thinks we're country superstars," Paloma adds.

Barney shakes his head. "Not anymore, but now I know there's something more to it. You two are magical together. I have a knack for discovering the magical parts of things and people. Like this town," he says, gesturing around the bar and probably all of Frostpine Hollow before continuing, "it's got unique ways of bringing people together from all kinds of walks of life. I met my late wife here. She never planned to stay more than a day."

"Call it kismet?" Paloma giggles.

He shrugs. "Something like that. A snowstorm kept her here for another day, and we just kept bumping into each other until we decided it was enough and to introduce ourselves."

"Cute," I offer, wondering if he's trying to get us to talk about how Paloma and I met.

"Indeed," Barney agrees. He leans back and grabs a remote, switching one of the TVs above us to the weather channel. I knew that the weather was getting bad, but not like *that*. What we're seeing unfold is a winter storm about to hit the state. About to hit *this* town.

"Fuck," I groan, eyes widening. Barney waves his hand, dismissing any worry that's creeping in already.

"You'll be alright as long as you leave soon. It's going to truly hit us in a few hours. I'd just try to get back to wherever you're staying, though. Don't wait around the square." Barney goes to the fridge, pulls out two water bottles, and hands them to us. It doesn't seem like the weather on the TV is fazing anyone else in the bar, so it kind of feels like we're in a bubble with Barney learning about this winter storm. Or the twilight zone.

The hairs on the back of my neck stand and I'm starting to feel off. Damn, Barney and his talk about magic and feeling like this town does things to people.

I will not end my story in a town called Frostpine Hollow. Absolutely not, I refuse to.

"We should go, I'm ready," I speak up, already mentally making sure I have the car keys, my wallet, and my phone.

Paloma smiles and holds onto the water bottles for us before glancing at me. "You don't want to play darts anymore?"

I shake my head, and Barney gives me a look. *Stop looking at me, old Wizard!*

"No, I'm not in the mood anymore. Super tired now all of a sudden."

The fact that Paloma isn't freaking out at all about the snowstorm when she hates the cold and snow even more…

I really am in the twilight zone if she's not panicking and *I am.*

Shit. It's starting.

Graham: 1

Paloma: 1

Winter storm and Old Wizard: 1000+

The wind outside finally reveals itself as the window panes shake, and some of the patrons gasp. *Finally!* Paloma jumps a little and she seemingly starts to realize what Barney has been talking about this whole time and what I've been silently losing my shit over.

"Wow, that was strong. Winter storm, you say?" she squeaks out and takes a step back.

"He looks like he could drive through the chaos," Barney assures Paloma and throws me a wink.

In that fucking boxcar? Sure, old man. I just give him a curt nod and grab Paloma's elbow gently, ready to pull her to the entrance.

"It was nice meeting you, Barney. Hope to see you again," she calls out as we both begin to move our feet.

He smiles widely and touches his right hand to his heart. "Thank you for the song. I feel Carol right here." He taps his chest. "It was nice meeting y'all. Come back for some of my famous moonshine or for another karaoke song. Don't be a stranger."

"We won't," I finally tell him and make sure she has everything she came with before we're walking outside. The wind hits us like knives, and she's instantly huddling closer to me. I don't mind wrapping my body around her again as we make our way to the car. The snow is starting to fall heavier than what was forecasted for this hour on TV. It won't take us long to make it back to the cabin, even if I drive slow and careful.

But what makes me worry is tomorrow. Will we be trapped in the cabin for the remainder of our trip? What if we can't get back to the airport on time? What if Colbie doesn't get her songs?

The spiraling questions fill my head as Paloma naps in the passenger seat. I'm no stranger to being snowed in. Granted, it was in my home whenever Nashville had horrible winter storms that lasted like four days and no snowplows to clear the streets—the downside of living in a hilly neighborhood.

But the main spiraling thought that keeps me alert the last few minutes of the drive back: how the hell will I survive being snowed in with Paloma?

Paloma

CHAPTER ELEVEN

I HAD the weirdest dream that Graham carried me from the car to my bed and tucked me in. But not before he laid a soft kiss on my forehead. I woke up feeling a bit confused, delusional, and thirsty.

The water bottle Barney gave me is on my nightstand, and I sit up, downing it quickly. The cabin is quite save for the heater humming throughout the place, but I can't hear Graham at all. Is he still sleeping? The clock on the nightstand says 7:30 a.m., so I wouldn't put it past him to still be in bed. Besides, he drove us all the way back while it snowed, and I was barely conscious for the damn ride. I was hoping to be his hype man if he needed me, but the moment my head hit the headrest, I was out.

I decide to push the covers off and head to the window to see the damage from last night's winter storm. The moment I pull the heavy curtains back, I gasp. All I see is *white*.

Shit. We're snowed in, there's no doubt about it.

I briefly thank past versions of ourselves for getting groceries before this happened. I don't even want to know what I'd have to eat to survive if we didn't. Probably just the remnants of spices

70

the place had for guests and nothing else. Nothing like lemon pepper seasoning for breakfast. Yum.

After I get ready for the morning and change into a sweat suit, I make my way to the kitchen and start the coffee machine, putting in enough for if Graham wants some too. I find myself leaning my ear against his door to check for any signs of life before I barge in, but I hear his soft snoring. I decide to be nice and let him sleep in a bit while I make us coffee, then some breakfast later once he's up.

By the time I've got my coffee in hand and situated myself in front of the windows in the living room, I'm watching the snow continue to fall. It's mesmerizing and calming as I sip on my coffee. I think back to last night and how much fun it was, but also how much it felt like my emotions were being pulled this way and that.

I sang the very specific song on stage because I was being petty and needed to send him a message. I think he got it, but the way he went from Grinch to Saint Nick in a single second was quite irritating. The thoughts continue to loom around my mind before I sigh and put my coffee down on a nearby counter and head to the coffee table to grab my journal and pen. A melody is already starting to form in my head as I think of Barney, the bar, and Graham.

I start to let the memories flood in and allow the emotions to come up instead of pushing them down. The writing process is unique for everyone, but for me, it's allowing myself to remember the pain, the hurt, and everything in between. I could probably write ten songs based on how things have been going since our first meeting with Loren a few days ago, but I focus on last night and how it made me feel.

The pen moves swiftly along the page, pieces of my heart scattering in dark ink. Everything starts to flow like it used to, and I've missed it.

I smile to myself, wondering how Montrose would react not

only to knowing I haven't given the label a current song in ages, but that I'm finally writing because of this damn EP. Because of Graham.

The pen scrapes against the page as I finish the last verse and look at what I've created. I don't think I've written a song *that* fast before. Granted, it will need some polishing, but that's why a first draft is a first draft.

It will have a catchy chorus and holiday vibes, but it isn't quite a romantic song. It's got heart and soul, but it's more of a song about confusion, lingering feelings, and wondering if there's more to the story about how things were left. My eyes gloss over the page once more, stuck on one of the verses toward the end of the song.

I can see a ghost in those green eyes

Graham doesn't open up when he's right in front of you. He doesn't get intimate like that and doesn't prefer pillow talk. He likes to reach into the crevices of his heart through his writing, and I've always wondered how he can live like that. It makes communicating with him so damn hard unless you stick him in a studio and force him to write out his feelings for you to read or hear.

He's a hard soul to crack, and I've only been a witness to it a few times. Even during our relationship, it felt like I couldn't quite know what he was feeling unless we worked on a song together at Indigo Roots. Sometimes I took to blame how things ended because I didn't push him to be honest with me, but I've spent enough time wallowing in my own grief over the relationship to know that I wasn't just to blame. He didn't communicate —didn't work on himself for the betterment of *us*.

After rereading the lyrics from the journal, I lean over, grab Lucie, which has been resting on the couch, and start humming and playing some chords to match the melody in my head. I start to feel the song come more to life, and it makes me smile and my stomach flutter in the best way. I'm in love with songwriting and there's no denying it. My soul thrives in this.

A cleared throat interrupts my strumming, and I almost jump out of my skin, snapping my neck to see Graham holding a cup of coffee, leaning against one of the wooden beams that enter the living room. He's got on a wrinkled white shirt and even more wrinkled grey sweatpants. He clearly just rolled out of bed.

"I didn't hear you," I say, stopping my strumming and placing my guitar pick on my thigh.

"You seemed to be in the zone. I didn't want to bother you. Surprised you didn't hear me in the kitchen, though. I almost dropped the creamer."

I shake my head. "Didn't hear anything, which surprises me. A robber could've broken inside and I wouldn't have even known."

This makes Graham laugh. "I think you'd notice and have enough time to throw your guitar at him."

"Not my Gibson!" I counter, clutching her close to my chest. My most prized possession. I don't know what I'd do without her.

He nods. "Yep... Sorry to break your heart, Sugarplum. Only thing in reach to protect us."

"And where are you in this whole scenario?" I ask, eyes staying on him as he moves about the living room, until he finally takes a seat next to me. He eyes my journal, and my hand is fast to reach over and snap it closed. He doesn't say a thing, but I can almost read his mind.

"Snoozing away like a bear in hibernation."

"You did snore a lot this morning," I add. He smirks before nudging my knee with his. The guitar sways in my lap, and I giggle.

"I don't snore."

"Then what did I hear?"

He thinks for a moment. "Maybe you're hearing things. Could be the old cabin… It's haunted."

My eyes widen. "Don't say that! You know I don't like that kinda stuff."

"Right. I forgot you're not a horror fanatic like me."

Graham could watch a million scary movies and never break a sweat or have a nightmare. It's concerning, no doubt. I can't imagine not being able to go into a dark alley or even a dark room and *not* think the worst will happen or a demon will come out and grab you.

He leans in so close that I can see little specs of yellow in his irises, and my heart thumps harder in my chest. He smells like aftershave, minty toothpaste, and a hint of coffee. And some musky cologne. He smells like *Graham*.

His lips twist into a smile and I can't take my eyes off them. Despite the words I've written today, they get pushed in this moment as I breathe him in and just remember the good we had. The amazing *nights* we've had years back. Does he still know how to do *that thing* he always did that made me even crazier for him?

"Did you hear me?" he repeats, and I look up into his eyes as I widen my own. Shit, was he talking this whole time? I was so transfixed by his lips.

"What?" I softly ask. He smiles before leaning back, and I miss the proximity of him instantly.

"I asked if you wanted to try out the hot tub. It's the perfect weather for it."

I look outside and my brows can't help but scrunch together. I turn to eye him incredulously. "You're joking, right? We'll get sick just from getting out all wet."

He pats my knee before standing up. I catch his eyes landing on my journal once more and I suddenly get protective over it. I grab it quickly and tuck it under my armpit before standing up to put my guitar back in its case.

"You'll be fine. I'll bring out hot chocolate, towels, and even some whiskey to warm us up."

"When the hell did you get time to get Whiskey?" I ask, looking around us and truly wondering if I blacked out for a day and he went on an adventure by himself.

"Barney slipped me some before we left. Figured we'd be sheltered in for a few days with this snow and wanted to bid us a fair well with some liquor."

"Oh, Barney." I sigh, shaking my head. That old man is trying to be a matchmaker of some sort just because he and his lover met in this town. Graham and I didn't even meet here!

"Come on," Graham exclaims, waving me over. "It'll be nice to just soak in the tub and not work. Then we can tackle a few songs and then record them for Colbie. Figure sending her lyric sheets and voice memos will do us some good while we're stuck here."

I nod, but not before I add, without realizing, "I know a few other things that will do us some good."

Graham stills before his eyebrows shoot up. "What?"

I smirk, walking up to him and patting his chest before continuing on my way to the stairs to change into my bathing suit. "I was talking about watching Christmas movies and eating some popcorn with Valentina, Graham."

His cheeks turn bright red before he nods and rushes over to his bedroom door. He looks back at me and nods again, his mind clearly short-circuiting from my suggestive words. "R-right," he manages to say before going into his room and slamming the door.

Graham: 1

Paloma: 2

This is getting *fun*.

GRAHAM WAS RIGHT, which is a rare occurrence. The hot tub feels amazing and the view is something out of a wildlife magazine. It makes it seem unreal, but it's right there in front of me. The wildlife is quiet for a bit as the snow slows, so we come out to the deck at the perfect moment.

Graham passes me a bottle of whiskey, and I take a small sip, letting it warm my body, then hand it back to him, our hands grazing.

He's wearing dark blue swim trunks, and funny enough, the only bikini I packed was my navy blue one with white bows scattered across the fabric. Of course we're matching. How jolly.

"So what did you do this morning? Write a new song or just find a melody?" He breaks the silence we've been in, but it wasn't an uncomfortable one. We were enjoying the hot tub and scenery around us, and sipping the whiskey.

"Both," I admit. He nods, and he looks like he wants to ask more, but he stays quiet. I take this chance to be the one to talk. "Any lyrics coming to mind for you while we've been here?"

That's when he glances at me, his striking green eyes taking hold of everything I possess. "A few, but I don't know if they'd come together well."

"Like what?" I ask, moving a bit closer to reach for the whiskey that seems to be warming my body, and I want more of it. It's also giving me the liquid courage to ask Graham more questions, so I don't see it as a bad thing.

What else are you supposed to do when snowed in with your ex?

He clears his throat before snatching the whiskey from me. He takes a sip and then presses his lips tightly together. My hand lingers in the air still from when he took the bottle from me before it settles on the hot tub. He doesn't say anything, but he inches a bit closer so we're about a foot apart now, knees almost touching.

"You can tell me," I whisper, hoping he knows that whatever he says in this cabin can stay in this cabin if he wants it to. He sighs, leaning his head back and looking up at the ceiling of the deck above us. I inch closer, resting my hand on his shoulder. He jumps a little from the contact, but stays put and doesn't move his eyes from above.

He finally speaks up. "I did some things that I regret, Paloma. Things I wish I could take back."

"Like with family? With Stetson? Work?" I ask, wanting to be there for him. Maybe he can't talk about it with anyone else and having me here is helping him finally speak it into existence.

He shakes his head. "No, not quite. It's a bit more complicated than that. It's just some dumb decisions that I feel changed the course of everything in my life because of how naive I was."

"Wow, Frostbite doesn't think he's still naive?" I joke, but he doesn't laugh. I squeeze his shoulder, and he finally looks down and locks eyes with me.

"I think I've changed since we last spoke." It's not a question, it's a statement. Something he's convinced himself is true. Is it? Has he truly changed?

"I haven't known this Graham long enough to know if that's true," I counter, leaning in a bit more. The whiskey is coursing through me and it's giving me a bit more confidence than I usually have. The cold doesn't help, making me want to get closer to him and cuddle for warmth. The hot tub can be turned up a bit, but who wants that when you've got a tall country man with body heat to warm a house?

"I've missed the way we were, but I'm also happy to know where we are now," Graham says.

"Where are we now?" I ask.

He chews on his bottom lip before replying. "In better places. More mature. More grown. We still make mistakes, but I'm sure we react better to them now than we did before."

I cock my head to the side as I listen to him. We have grown and gotten more mature over the years, but I'm still confused about why he's bringing this up. Especially if he's talking about mistakes he's made in the past. I wish he'd just spit it out.

"What are you hiding? Or running from?" The words spill out of my lips before I can stop them. His hand underwater reaches for my leg, grasping it gently, but the action makes my stomach flip.

"I can't bear to truly lose you, Paloma."

"What do you mean? Are you running from me?"

He shakes his head. "No, but you will run from me once you hear what I did."

"Just spit it out, Graham," I say a bit louder. I grab his hand underwater and try to rip it off my thigh, but he doesn't move. I glare at him, huffing out a loud breath. The irritation for Graham Westin comes back in full swing.

"I don't want to hurt you. I already did when we ended things."

"When *you* ended things," I blatantly remind him. My hand tightens around his underwater, but he doesn't budge.

"Yes, when I ended things," he corrects himself. I let go of his hand, giving up, but I lean in a bit closer to him. His eyes dance around my face before settling on my lips.

"That was in the past, Graham. I don't know why we're talking about it like it'll matter what you say or apologize for. It happened, we happened. It ended. We're working together on this EP and then we'll be back to our own lives in a few days."

"But it does matter," he starts again. I roll my eyes, and his hand lifts from my thigh. I almost miss the feeling of it, but I push that thought away.

"Then. Just. Say. It." The words are loud and echo around us as I look at him sternly.

Instead of saying what he's been trying to avoid, he does the worst thing possible.

Graham kisses me.
And I let him.

Graham
CHAPTER TWELVE

I KISSED Paloma and I don't regret a single thing. Especially when she doesn't push me away and kisses me back. The hot tub is steaming around us, and the snow is starting back up again while we stay locked to each other.

My hands are all over her. Her hair, her hips, her thighs, and then her face. I hold her like I'm going to lose her, and her hands are on my shoulders, chest, and then my neck, pulling me closer to her.

"Graham," she moans between kisses.

"Sorry," I say out of breath once we separate. She shakes her head before biting her lip and pulling me in again for a few more kisses. A *please* comes out of my lips and I can't believe it does. It only riles Paloma up more to keep kissing me.

I know kissing her was the worst thing I could've done instead of just telling her the truth, but I couldn't. I don't know if I'm ready yet. She deserves to know, but I don't want to lose her in the aftermath.

When she asked me if I'd thought of anything to write about since we've been on this trip, or even since seeing each other in the conference room with Loren, I lied.

I've had so many lyrics and melodies come to mind that have been in the background, I haven't allowed myself to be lured in and put to paper or guitar. My journal hasn't begged for my attention this much in a while. My fingers itch for my pen just like it's itching to feel every curve on Paloma's body. She's straddling me now, our cores almost touching. Just out of reach. There's no doubt that she can feel how turned on I've become.

A sound comes out of Paloma's lips and her doe eyes are half-lidded, making me want to get her out of this hot tub and into the cabin. Preferably to my bedroom.

"Talk to me, Sugarplum," I whisper, pressing my fingers into her thighs, stomach, anywhere it can find purchase.

She takes a deep breath before she chews the inside of her cheek. She's nervous, and I am too. The wind howls around us, and we both jump. Her legs are quick to get off me, and I almost pull her back onto me.

"We should head inside," she whispers before standing up and fixing her bikini from where I was grabbing and pulling. She then tries to run her hands through her wet strands, but it's almost impossible. Her cheeks turn red, and I look away for a moment.

"Right, we can go. You'd have to get out first. The towels are right at the steps."

"You sure?" she asks. I glance at her for a moment and nod. I look down at my crotch before her cheeks turn even redder.

"Yeah, please." I chuckle.

"I'll go." She almost laughs before climbing out and pulling a towel around her body. I'm right after her, making sure to get the towel as quickly as I can to cover my growing erection. We're running inside the cabin at the speed of light until we almost slip into each other from our wet feet.

"Fuck!" I yelp, trying to hold onto the air for balance, but I go down. I hear her in front of me also fall with a big *oof* escaping her lips before we're down for the count. A stream of giggles follow, and I lean up to look at her a couple feet away.

"We should've thought about that better." I laugh alongside her. Paloma's hair is all over her shoulders and face as she tries to move it and secure it into a wet bun above her head.

"Didn't really think about the hardwood floors running inside," she exclaims. I get up carefully and do my best to walk over to her, reaching my hand out. My body is covered in goosebumps from the hot tub and the sudden chill of the weather outside. The heat inside the cabin is starting to warm me up, but not fast enough. She's right that we might get sick from this spontaneous adventure.

"Thanks," she says, grabbing onto my hand. I pull her up, but her feet slip again, and I grab her waist, causing my towel to drop in the process. The movement of my grip on her pulls her into my chest and my crotch basically stabs her lower belly in the process.

"Shit, sorry," I mumble out, trying to get her to balance on her own two feet while trying to push her away from me as best as I can.

"Whoa." Her eyes widen as she feels what I was hoping she didn't need to feel today. This is wrong and I shouldn't be thinking about my ex like this. We're exes for a reason. Nothing good comes from getting back with an ex, at least that's what I've been told.

I take a step back once we find our footing before slipping out another apology. "I shouldn't have kissed you," I add. I grab the towel from the ground and wrap it around my torso once more before begging the horny gods to give me deliverance and let my erection settle. It doesn't help seeing her in this state with a glistening chest, red cheeks, and disheveled wet hair already coming out of its bun.

She's beautiful, and I can't imagine taking my eyes off her.

All the regret comes up to my throat like a thick log, reminding me of the shit I put her through.

"It's okay, Graham," she finally breathes out. She hugs the towel closer to her before she heads down the hall toward the stairs.

"Dinner for lunch?" I ask, watching her turn around. She nods and smiles.

"Yeah. And Graham?" Her words halt me in my walk to my room. I raise a brow and cock my head, waiting for her to continue. "I kissed you back. It wasn't just you."

Oh.

WE'RE EATING STEAK, mashed potatoes, and parmesan-crusted asparagus while we watch a Christmas movie about a man's ghost of Christmas past. We're on barstools in the kitchen, watching it at an angle with the TV loud as we eat quietly. While I cooked the steak, she made the rest, and it turned out so delicious. I forgot how well we work in the kitchen together.

"This part is my favorite," Paloma speaks up, nodding toward the TV. I watch the scene and laugh with her.

"That is a good one," I reply, grabbing my glass of water and chugging. I eye my journal on the coffee table from afar, and my fingers itch for it. The rest of my food gets inhaled, and I grab her plate after she finishes and rinse them both off before placing them in the dishwasher.

"Want to finish the movie or begin writing?" Paloma asks, hopping off her barstool and heading for the living room. She plops down on the couch and keeps her eyes on the TV.

"You can keep watching it. I might write some." This catches her attention and she cranes her neck to look back at me.

"Really?"

"Mhm," I hum, "but keep the TV going, I can write with it on. It won't distract me."

"Sure thing," she replies, grabbing the remote and turning it down a bit, and I grab my journal, then realize I don't have a pen here. It's probably in my case or bedroom.

"Shit, forgot my pen, I'll be right back."

"Just use mine, unless you have something against pink glittery pens."

I laugh. "No, not at all. I'll gladly use it. Might write so much I use all the ink."

She gives me a warm smile. "Okay, Frosty," she says before turning her attention back to the TV.

Once I have everything I need, I head to the chair Paloma was sitting on earlier this morning and face the big windows, watching the snow continue to fall. I make a mental note to find a shovel and start clearing the snow before it melts with the sun and freezes overnight. The last thing we need is to encounter black ice when we try to get out of the cabin for any reason. I'd totally dominate Paloma in a snowball fight.

I close my eyes for a moment, allowing myself to get into my mind and find the way to open my heart and emotions the way I've been wanting to all week. My fingers twiddle with the pen and I open my eyes, ready to start. The page starts to fill with words that don't make sense, don't rhyme, and it's more of a word vomit than a song. But that doesn't matter. What matters is that I'm *writing*. My thoughts are turning into words and I feel a bit better.

I flip the page and start to think about Paloma and our predicament here. Not just being snowed in, but the fact that we have to write an EP together, we have unspoken words we need to vocalize, and some feelings that are starting to resurface on my end.

There's no denying that I loved Paloma with all my heart, but things were in the way, and I had to grow up. How does one tell someone that? Second chances don't come easy, and I don't even know if I want it and I certainly know I don't deserve it.

She can find someone better who can offer her the things I once couldn't. I can now, but why should she settle for that? It's not fair.

My thoughts are moving too fast for the pen as I start writing lyrics that actually make sense. The melody is strong in my mind, and I want to take out my guitar and start making it into music, but I force myself to stick to the lyrics for now. This was never my strongest suit and I want to lean into it this time. Paloma was always the better one in this department.

I reread the first verse and I swallow the thickness in my throat.

I don't think I like
The way we're so stuck on this high
Tried so hard to forget you
But it just turned my heart blue

The words are prominent and stare at me like the end of a barrel. Forcing me to face my feelings—face the music. I keep writing and find a good chorus to match the first verse.

And you say we're fine
To walk on this dangerous line
And my heart's on fire
It's at a crossroad I cannot define

Because I'm so confused about what I want to do next. I'm terrified of what will come after this work trip. Will we go back to being strangers? Or will we be able to work our way back to being friends, and then hopefully to something more?

I'm at a crossroads of what ifs.

I sigh loudly, and Paloma makes a noise before I turn to see her getting up and stretching. The movie is over, credits rolling on the screen, and I can't believe I tuned it out that much.

"I'm going to start finding a melody for another song," she states, grabbing her guitar, and I nod, focusing back on my journal. The next verse comes to me easily as I hear her strumming. Surprisingly, it doesn't distract me from the melody that's already curating in my mind.

I don't think it's fair
To say I never cared
It's impossible to write down
All the feelings kept around

Paloma starts to hum, and her voice fills my ears, and I lean into it, closing my eyes for a moment. Her voice is magical and can transport me to another world just by humming.

I try to refocus and work on a bridge, but it doesn't fit for this song. I play the song in my head once more before settling on a post-chorus verse.

There's times I thought I'd hate you
But it's just not true…

There. One song written. It feels like a heavy weight has been lifted from my shoulders and I audibly let out a shaky breath. It's not for the EP, but it's allowed me to process some of the thoughts that have been lingering.

Can't write new songs unless you filter out the old ones stuck in your heart. I get up and turn the chair back around to face Paloma, and she looks up from her guitar.

"Good writing session?"

I nod and wiggle my journal in the air. "Finally wrote something."

"Nice, is it something for the EP or just for you?"

"Just for me," I say slowly. I want to apologize if she thought I was working on something for the EP, but I hold back. It's like she sees it on my face, though, because she speaks up.

"That's okay! I wrote a song this morning and feel way better. Like I was able to get out some thoughts that needed to be written before I could continue on this EP."

"Exactly," I agree, offering another smile. Her eyes sparkle as she returns it and then goes back to strumming. "That's a good tune, I think I have the perfect line to start us off," I add.

"Go for it, Frosty," she giggles, continuing to strum with her glittery purple pick.

I open a new page in my journal and get to writing before I sing it out for Paloma to hear.

Paloma

CHAPTER THIRTEEN

WE WRITE two more songs in a span of three hours and get them voice-recorded as well. That makes three songs done for the EP.

It felt much easier today than it did at the beginning of this trip, but I think it's because of the state we're in. We haven't seen each other in years, haven't written together in a while, and we're exes.

That last part has been circling my brain for the last hour as we finish up a late dinner and work together to tidy up the place. Cleaning helps me settle my brain for the night, and I'm glad that Graham didn't protest. I'm starting to like being in his company, despite the weather forcing us to.

It does seem to be getting a bit chillier, too, with the sun down, but the house is very *quiet* as we finish cleaning up, and I'm ready for my night routine. I want to make some tea with a peppermint tea box I found in one of the cabinets, so I was lingering in the kitchen when I noticed the sound.

"Graham?" I ask slowly, turning to see him finishing rinsing the sink from his washing duties.

"Hm?" His hum is louder than normal, and it makes me really curious why I'm honing in on this.

"Is it quieter or is it just me?"

Graham takes this moment to glance at me before standing still and listening. No humming. No whirring. *Nothing*.

"Huh," he grunts, shaking his head.

"What? What is it?" I ask, getting closer to him. I forgot my slippers upstairs, so when I glide my feet closer to him, I notice the hardwood floor is a bit colder too. I almost gasp at the sudden change.

"I think the heater stopped. I'll go check the thermostat down the hall. Wait here," he replies, already in go mode. I barely know a thing or two about the HVAC system in my place with Lacey. So, to offer any guidance on a *house,* especially in this caliber, I felt out of my element. I gladly let Graham take care of it as I hurry to make my tea. If anything else goes wrong, like the electricity zonking out on us, I'd at least like to make sure my tea is hot and ready to warm me up tonight.

I glance quickly at the fireplace and wonder if that's something we can use last resort. Does Graham know how to start a fire? Do we even have wood? The thoughts are circling my brain for a moment before I hear a loud *Fuck*.

"Whoa, language!" I spit out.

Graham is veering back into view as he runs his hands through his hair and his eyes are wide. He takes a deep breath before resting his hands on his hips. "The heater broke, most likely with the storm and heavy snow. I'll go check in the basement to see if there is anything I can do."

I don't have time to respond as he gives me a quick look and walks away. My body aches to help in any way I can, but I can feel my brain pause. What can I do that Graham isn't already trying to take charge with? When we were together, he took care of a lot of things that went wrong in either of our homes. It was definitely one thing Lacey missed when we broke up—having a man around to do the maintenance.

The only thing I can think of right now is making him a mug of tea, in case he needs it. As I prepare that, the place starts to get colder by the minute. It only takes a few minutes for the tea to be ready, and I quickly grab my boots to wear indoors. I hate wearing shoes inside, but I don't know how long we'll be without heat.

Graham returns a few minutes later, and the expression on his face tells me there isn't any good news. I raise a brow and wrap my arms around my chest to keep my body heat intact.

"Well?" I ask, chewing the inside of my cheek raw.

"It's definitely broken. It'll need maintenance and I can text Montrose to get a hold of the owner, but I doubt they'd send anyone right now."

It's starting to snow some more from what I can see through the window and it worries me what's to come.

"Can we go anywhere? Maybe there's a hotel room available we can go to near Barney's bar?"

Graham chuckles nervously and shakes his head. "We won't even make it out of the road with that boxcar Montrose got us. We're stuck here inevitably, Sugarplum."

"Inevitably? Oh come on," I reply, attempting to keep down a shiver, but it's too late, and my body gives in and my teeth chatter. Graham studies me for a second before it looks like there's a lightbulb that flicks on in his head.

"Maybe until our trip is over, but I think we can use that fireplace." He points to it, and I nod, shuffling my boots closer to it in the living room.

"What do you need me to do?" I ask, wanting to help in any way. "I made you tea to warm up," I add.

He smiles. "Thank you, I'll definitely need it with how cold the basement already got. We might need to use that sauna while we have power."

"I don't think that'd be a great idea, we'd get sick the moment we stepped out," I remind him. That would be the worst thing. Getting snowed in *and* sick? No, thank you.

"Right. You're right," he responds with a nod. He presses his lips tightly together, looking around the room before his eyes widen. "Go see if there are any cardboard boxes or magazines you can rip up so we can start a fire. And look for matches! I'll look for wood; they have to have some stored away for their guests."

I nod, ready to get into action and follow Graham's directions. He immediately runs out of the living room to who knows where, and I start gathering any magazines or papers I can find to discard, as well as any pantry boxes from our grocery haul. After I find a small box of matches in one of the drawers, I start to rip them up near the fireplace and set the pieces in a box nearby while Graham returns, arms full of logs. The smile that pours from both of our faces can light up this room if the power went out.

"You found some!" I exclaim, clapping my hands a bit. He lays the logs down in a huff before scratching his head and then opening the metal doors and then toggling with something. "What's that?" I ask.

He glances at me as he continues to toggle with it, as well as moving his hand inside the fireplace before responding. "The fireplace damper. You have to make sure it's open before starting a fire. Don't want to flood the house with smoke and carbon monoxide. I'm feeling for a draft too, to double-check it's open."

"I can feel it already," I say, feeling the bits of wind from the chimney flowing through the fireplace.

"Hand me the matches, please," Graham asks after he puts some logs onto the grate. I find the box and hand it to him, watching him grab some ripped-up cardboard boxes I laid before us, and he lights one before placing it gently under the logs. He repeats this process for a bit, then fans out the fire with another piece.

"Making sure there's enough oxygen for the fire to grow," he notes, focusing on the growing flames. "Even if we're here for a bit, the smolder will keep burning long after we run out of logs to add."

I appreciate him teaching me and I take it all in. I study Graham in his element for a while, admiring his facial features. He turns his head for a bit, catching me, and my face instantly heats, and it's not because of the fire.

"You okay?" he asks softly, adding a bit more pieces of ripped paper under the logs.

I nod. "Yep, just peachy. Perfect. Amazing." The words spill out before I can stop them.

He chuckles, shifting his legs to a different seating position. "What's on your mind, Sugarplum?"

I ponder for a moment, enjoying the growing sounds of the crackling fire that's before us. "I like being here with you," I finally confess.

"Oh, yeah? Finally growing soft on me?" he jokes. I lean in to nudge his arm with my fist.

"Oh, shut up. You know what I mean! I really like knowing that we're in this predicament together."

He's quiet as he focuses on the fire and then to me. His jaw clenches and I can see his Adam's apple bob as he swallows. "Are you admitting that you broke the heater just so we can spend a cold night together?"

I roll my eyes and laugh. "No! Not that, silly." I take a deep breath. "It's nice having you know how to check for the heater, build this fire, and keep me warm."

There's silence around us again and I gulp, wanting to take back my confession the more the silence grows. But then he smiles and leans back from the fireplace, closer to me. I can smell bits of smoke on him and his usual scent. The one I love smelling. I close my eyes for a bit and inhale it all.

"It's nothing, Paloma. I'd do this every night for you if I had to."

I open my eyes and he's staring at me. No, not my eyes. He's staring at my lips. He licks his own and clears his throat before traveling his eyes up to mine. The reflection of the fire against his irises is beautiful. He's beautiful. The pain of the past and how we ended things is pushed away so easily with those green eyes.

I bask in the feeling a bit longer, letting my body react to him in the ways I've been trying to ignore.

"Paloma…" he whispers, leaning in a bit more. I do too. My legs are starting to get colder the longer I stay on the floor with him, but I don't care. The fire is starting to warm up the living room, and hopefully it'll spread throughout the house in no time.

"Graham," I say his name with an exhale, hoping it can still my rapid beating heart.

We don't have to say anything else. The kiss in the hot tub flashes back and I wanted more in that moment. More of him. More of what we're becoming in this cabin work trip. This getaway from reality.

I lean in more, reaching my palm out to touch his chin. He leans into the touch and closes his eyes for a moment before he drops the piece of cardboard he was holding.

"Fuck it," he whispers before wrapping his hands around my cheeks and pulling me in for a kiss.

Graham

CHAPTER FOURTEEN

HER SOFT LIPS press against mine as I pull her in closer. I can't describe the feeling of her against me right here in this moment. Ultimate bliss.

She lets out a soft moan, and it drills into my brain, sparking my neurons and my body to react to her. I instantly move my hands down to her hips, then under her knees to drag her on top of me. She's straddling me with ease and holds onto the back of my neck as we continue to kiss. Her hair cascades over us with our movements, and all I smell is *her*. I want to drown in her.

There's a random buzzing that pulls us away for a moment, and we both look around the fire-lit room as my phone lights up with a call. I let it ring, but then once it ends, Paloma's phone starts to light up as well with a call. I feel her fingers wrap around my chin to pull my attention back to her.

"They can wait," she whispers, her brown eyes like embers under the glow of the fire. She's beautiful, iridescent, and every word in the dictionary that would simply show her picture if you looked it up.

"They can," I reply softly, pulling her in tightly again, letting her swallow me whole with not just her lips but her hair, her scent, and everything Paloma.

The kisses are deep, longing, and something I didn't know I was missing until this moment. It was an inkling I felt in the hot tub, but this has magnified by a million.

My hands are all over her as well, gliding up and down her waist and slowly drifting my fingers under her shirt. Her skin is soft, sparking electricity all over my body, and it's embarrassing to admit how fast I'm getting an erection from just this.

She moans for a bit in the kiss, and I drag my teeth over her bottom lip, biting and pulling. This makes her squeal a little louder and her legs tighten around my waist. She circles her hips, and my fingers tighten, sure to leave bruises tomorrow.

The reminder that when we were together, that was something she liked. Paloma doesn't like controlling or possessive men, but she does like knowing how riled up and needy she makes a man. She loved when I grabbed her hard enough to leave indents on her hips, waist, or thighs. Like she wants to see them the next morning and be reminded of what happened. That, for a moment, she was someone's. Mine.

"Please," she pleads in a soft breath, grinding against me once more. My hands move higher and I feel the fabric of her bra. I pull back a bit from the kiss, and she's panting, cheeks red and eyes sparkling. A look I can't say no to.

"Are you sure?"

She nods. "It's not like we haven't before."

I stare at her for a moment and there's a weight on my chest. The feeling of resentment toward the past me and my mistakes. Of pushing her away when I should've pulled her closer.

"But we're different people now. So much has changed between us, Paloma," I say, brushing my fingertips along the band of her bra. The movement grounds me, so I keep doing it.

Her brows scrunch together and her eyes stay on mine. It looks like there's a million questions running through her mind and I don't blame her. She thinks I'm pushing her away again, but I'm honestly trying to keep the lines uncrossed.

She sighs and adjusts herself so she's still straddling me, but a bit lower on my waist so she's not directly grinding me. Not directly over my erection anymore.

"Paloma?" I ask, moving my fingers to squeeze her right under the bra band.

"What aren't you telling me?"

"What do you mean?"

She takes this moment to slide off me, and it feels like glass shattered and our little cabin bubble has broken. That reality has set in. My stomach drops and my breathing gets a bit hard.

She crosses her arms over her chest as she heads to one of the couches, but she doesn't sit down on it—just slides to the floor with her back up against it. We're feet away, but it feels like galaxies apart.

I swallow the thick wad of cotton in my throat. "Talk to me, Paloma."

Her eyes finally find mine and they're glossy. "You've been weird since our meeting with Loren and it feels like I was able to see the walls fall while being here, but there's still some stiffness to you. I can't put my finger on it."

This is the part where I break her heart—again. Isn't it? Where she finds out everything I've been hiding, and I lose the one person I've truly cared about in my life. Stetson pushed me so many times to tell her the truth, but I couldn't. Even he took a bit to forgive me, so I can't imagine her.

"It's just a lot of pressure from Montrose and Loren," I lie.

She shakes her head. "That's not it. Why won't you talk to me?"

"I am talking to you."

"No, you're not!" Her voice gets louder. She sighs again, dropping her head and pulling her knees to her chest. She looks so small from this distance, and I want to grab her and hold her until everything is better. Until she forgives me.

"You won't understand," I finally let out. She looks up, confusion etched across her face.

"I'm pressured just as much as you are. So it's something else. I can't keep working with you this week if this is how you'll be," she finally resorts. She starts to shift her body to get up, but I can't take it anymore.

Seeing her leave again will just break my fucking heart even more and she deserves better than this. She deserves the truth and if she hates me, then so be it.

"Wait," I call out. She stops midway, about to sit up. She looks at me and I see a tear cascade down her cheek. Fuck, she's so beautiful, and I hate seeing her like this. My Paloma.

What did she use to let me call her? My *cancioncita*. I call that nickname out, my Spanish horrible, but this gets her attention, and she sits back down.

"Spill," she states. I nod and scoot closer to where she is. I'm close to her spread out legs and when I touch her ankle, she lets me. I brush my fingers against her skin, and she takes a deep breath.

"I didn't break up with you because I got that songwriting contract."

There's silence. And then more silence. She doesn't say anything, just waits for me to explain. Her eyes go to me, then to the ground.

"The meeting went way differently that day than I explained it to you."

"Go on," she finally whispers.

"They wanted to talk to me about not just offering me a songwriting contract, but *us*."

"What do you mean? We were already writing songs together." She looks confused, and that hits me like a truck.

"We were, but under no contract that made sure we'd do it

together for the foreseeable future. They wanted Paloma and Graham. Not us separately. They wanted us to be a songwriting duo, officially."

She sucks in her cheeks, seemingly deep in thought, before she finally speaks up. "So what you're saying is that you kept me from the possibility of a great songwriting contract and decided to just get one yourself?"

Now I'm the one silent. Because she got it right. I selfishly got myself a contract instead.

"I was stupid and had a one-track mind," I state. "It doesn't make it better, Paloma. But I was young and didn't know what I was doing. I just wanted that deal so bad and wanted it for just *me*."

"So you lied to me!" Her voice cuts deep like a knife. "And why did I never get a call? A meeting from Montrose?"

That's when I know I'm going to get the worst of it all from her. I see her face crack, along with her heart, as the words pour out. "Because I told them that you weren't looking for a songwriting duo contract. That you wanted to go solo, too. I had a guitar case full of songs I wanted to spotlight that weren't duets. It was wrong, but I wanted to secure my career before Nashville chewed me up."

"And what about me? You tried to convince them to sign me as a single songwriter when you knew damn well we worked best as a duo?" This is when she finally stands up and runs her hands through her hair. She starts to laugh, and that's when I know she's at her breaking point. She turns around, looking at the windows, nothing but darkness outside.

"Paloma, I'm so sorry. Please believe me."

She whips around and shakes her head. "No, nothing you say to me will make it better. I've been so thankful to have a career in Nashville when we met and wrote beautifully. I thought the contract was the one thing, the one *sign* that meant I made it and

I should stay. Because all I would've wanted was to continue working with *you*, Graham."

"You've been writing amazing songs though," I offer, hoping I can repair things now that I've told her the truth.

She laughs once more. "No, I haven't. I can't even write a good solo song anymore. When we were together in the studio, I was going home writing all the songs I was able to. I collected a handful of lyrics to be able to hold myself from getting released from the contract for not having any songs to give the label."

My heart sinks. "So you haven't been writing since we ended things?"

She's quiet before nodding her head slightly. "Yeah." Her word is soft, barely audible. The fire cracking is louder than her.

"I can't be the sole reason you were able to write great songs, though." But I can't deny that it's the same for me too. I haven't been able to truly write from the heart since I did what I did and we went our separate ways. The *soul* of the songs isn't there anymore.

Having a muse really does make or break people in this industry. Paloma was mine, and I guess I was hers, too, without realizing.

"Yeah, Graham, you were," she finally confesses. "It's stupid to admit and I hate that it's even a thing to discuss at all. But something about you makes me a better writer. A better storyteller."

"I know you're mad at me," I start, and she sighs, flipping her hair over her shoulder before I continue, "I want to let you know that you brought life to my lyrics as well. It hasn't been the same without you, Sugarplum."

"Well, you fucked that up, didn't you, Frostbite?" She doesn't let me say anything else as she walks out of the living room and heads to the front door. I immediately get up and follow her.

"Where are you going? It's not safe outside," I call out as I watch her zip up a coat. She throws a beanie on for good measure before unlocking the door and pulling it open. The breeze almost pushes her back into my arms as I reach her. I try to grab the door, but she is faster than me, bolting outside and almost slipping.

"I need fresh air, please," she exclaims, heading down the stairs, and I flick on the porch light before putting on my own shoes and coat in record time to chase after her.

"Paloma!" I scream after her, my heart beating frantically against my chest. The wind is harsh and the flurries are blurring my vision as I try to follow her figure. She nears the car before whipping around.

"What? What else is there to say to me? You ruined everything and broke my heart and made me feel like all I did was wrong!" The tears are starting to fall down her cheeks like a waterfall and it breaks my fucking heart seeing her like this. It's a stark resemblance to the day we broke up.

"Please," I let out, reaching my hand out for her. The snow from last night has melted a bit in this morning's sun, so I know we're standing on sheets of ice with more snow packed on top. I don't want her to slip and hurt herself.

"Your ego got in the way of us and I can't believe I didn't see it from the start!" Paloma starts to walk to the side of the car, and that's when her foot slips out from under her, causing her to fall. I'm quick to jump after her to catch her, but my own feet slip on the snow-covered ice.

"Ah!" Paloma screams, and I let out a grunt as I grab her arm and try to pull her toward me. It's no use. We slide past the car and down the driveway into the darkness of the snow-capped mountains before us.

Paloma

CHAPTER FIFTEEN

MY ANKLE IS sore and everything is cold. My ass hurts and my arm feels like it's been stretched to its limit. But I'm alive, and it's all thanks to my number one enemy, Graham Westin.

He grabbed me just in time as I slipped, and even though I was in the heat of anger, it all came out as laughter the moment we finally stopped at the end of the driveway. It's dark all around us, save for the porch light up at the front door that seems so far away in this moment.

"You okay?" Graham asks, wrapping his other arm around me, his eyes wandering all over.

"Ankle hurts, but that's about it, thanks," I whisper. We stay like this, sitting on the cold, icy driveway as things from earlier come back to the forefront of my mind. The lie. The deceit Graham did to me. It hurt to finally realize what made him break up with me years ago.

I loved him so much, it felt like we were one and done. It was him for me. But then that night everything changed, and all because of him and his selfishness. My blood starts to boil again, despite the laughter still wanting to escape. At this point, I feel insane with how much I want to scream, laugh, and even cry.

"You look like you want to slap me but also cry," Graham slowly says, rubbing his hand down my arm. I shiver, my pants starting to soak from the ground.

"Honestly, Frosty, I want to do both," I tell him, huffing as I try to get up. It's hard since we can barely see our own footing, but I manage to stand. He follows suit, still holding onto me as if he's scared I'll slip away again.

"I give you full permission to, Paloma," he finally states as we start to walk back up the driveway as slowly and carefully as possible. I have boots on, but he looks like he tried to grab the closest pair and it's slippers. So he's having a tougher time getting back to the house.

"Here," I say as I start to pass him, holding my palm out, "grab my hand."

"Thanks." He wraps his cold, calloused hand around mine, and we make it back to the porch in one piece. He lets go, and I watch him shake his body, removing all the snow. I'm still at the bottom of the steps when I see the pile of soft snow next to me. I lean down and grab a fistful with my bare hands and throw it at his shoulder. It explodes and he gasps, turning swiftly toward me.

"You didn't."

"I did." I smile, placing my hands on my hips. He shakes his head and laughs.

"You asked for it. I was going to offer to make you hot chocolate, but not anymore," he says as he proceeds to step back down to grab some snow and throw it back. I attempt to jump out of the way, but it gets in my hair and I yelp.

"Graham!"

He throws his head back as laughter bubbles out of him. "Okay, I'm done!"

Graham starts to turn and walk back up the steps before I throw another one, aiming at his butt this time. He glances back at me, and I throw my hands up in surrender.

"Sorry!"

"Come on," he says, beckoning me with his hand. "I deserved that. I probably deserve an avalanche to hit me, but a snowball will suffice."

I roll my eyes as I head up the steps and we enter the home and he shuts the door. It's a bit warmer and cozier with the fire going. "Just make my hot chocolate and shut up."

I'm about to walk back to the living room when he grabs my elbow, stopping me. I turn to look up at him, his green eyes widening and his cheeks growing more rosy by the minute.

"Paloma, I really am sorry about how I was in the past. Trust me when I say that it was never my intention to hurt you. My ego got in the way of the best thing I already had in front of me. You. I don't want to screw it up again while we're here."

I'm quiet for a moment as I take in his words. I don't know if I can trust that they're genuine, though. I exhale loudly. "Graham, I don't know what to say. It'll take time to forgive you. You hurt me—songwriting is everything to me and your actions really took a toll on me and my passion."

"I never meant for it to. I understand that what I did affected you so deeply. Again, I am *so* sorry. I want to make it right by you, Paloma. Whether it takes me weeks, months, years, or even an eternity."

"We'd be dead by then," I giggle. His lips curve into a smile and my heart starts to give in just a bit. It feels like it's starting to warm up to him—or it's just the fireplace making me feel this way.

"Paloma, please," he whispers, leaning in. His hair is disheveled from the snowball and shaking it out and there's some water droplets hanging. One falls and hits my cheek. I get on my tiptoes, closing the space between us.

I might not have the heart to forgive him tonight, but maybe having him show me how truly sorry he is might make me feel a bit better.

"Show me," I say out loud in a single breath. His pupils enlarge and his lips twist as if he's trying to look for the right words to say. I don't let him speak as my hands reach up and grab his neck, pulling him into a kiss.

This kiss is different from the hot tub and the earlier one near the fireplace. It's a reconciliation kiss. His hands are soft, holding me like I'll break or run away, but I don't. I stay.

He bends a bit, his hands following his movements until they're behind my knees and yanking me up into an embrace. I wrap my legs around his waist, and he walks us through the house until we're in the living room, where it's the warmest, and he plops me down on the couch. He helps untie my boots before pulling the jacket off me. He doesn't let me lift a finger as he continues to undress me.

It's slow and intimate, his touch delicate and comforting. It reminds me of the times we had in the past, but this is much different. *He's* different and I can tell how much he's grown since I last saw him. Who he's been during this trip is the real Graham. Not the songwriter Graham Westin, who has to put on a show for everyone just to fit in.

Hell, I'm so different from who I was when we last spoke. Although I've barely written any new material until this work trip, I'm not the same girl he broke up with years ago.

Maybe what we needed was that break—the time apart to grow into who we need to be before we collided again.

"What are you thinking about?" Graham breaks my thinking and I almost laugh with how easy it is to just escape reality with him.

"Just this trip and you," I say in between kisses as he continues to undress me. He's got my shirt and pants off before he's starting to pull off his sweater and own sweatpants until he's standing in just his boxers. God, he's beautiful. Goosebumps rise on his skin with the cold, and so does mine, but he's quick to join me on the couch, hovering over me. He's got one leg relaxed on the couch while the other is haphazardly hanging off, trying to keep me in between. His erection pokes the inside of my thigh and I swallow hard.

"What about me?" he whispers, leaning in for another kiss and I let him. I breathe him in before responding. His fingers trace over my belly before going up and over the lines of my bra.

"The songs we wrote were so easy, despite our difficulties. Once we started, we didn't stop. I missed that spark."

His eyes stay on mine as his fingers hook around the bra strap. My breath stops for a moment, my heart seizing to beat. My cheeks are undoubtedly maroon with how badly I want him.

"Being with you makes me write like we used to," he slips out as he pulls the strap down my shoulder, moving to work on the other side.

"Yeah?" My hands reach for his chest and he shivers from the contact. He nods, groaning.

"Meeting you has changed me forever. I shouldn't have ever let you go."

The confession falls off his lips, and it makes my stomach do flips, my heart skip a beat, and everything else the human body does when it's unsure what to do with feelings and an intense need for someone.

"Graham," I rasp, unable to take it anymore. We almost pushed past the limits earlier before his secret came out, but now it feels like this is the right timing.

The universe has its way of doing that. Making sure you're in the right place at the right time when they're the right person. Maybe Frostpine Hollow does have that magic Barney was talking about. This snowstorm was supposed to happen to make us reveal our truths one way or another.

"Tell me what you want, Paloma," Graham whispers, his lips tickling my ear as he kisses it before placing kisses on my neck, shoulder, and then collarbone. I grab his shoulder and moan again.

"I want *you*, Graham. Now, tomorrow—"

"Next week?" He chuckles under his breath.

I want to roll my eyes, but the thought of that makes me not want to admit that *yes, I want that too.*

"Let's start with now," I respond. And before I can think of another word, he works fast to unclip my bra and massages my left breast before closing his lips around my nipple. I instantly let out a moan, drowning in the pleasure of what he knows to do with me.

It's been years, but it feels like no time has passed at all with us like this. We know this dance, the music of our bodies, and how to pleasure each other.

His tongue swirls along my nipple before he sucks a bit and pulls back. I hiss a bit from the movement before he wastes no time working on my right breast. He does the same thing and I can't help but grab onto his hair and pull, causing him to groan against my skin.

"Fuck, Graham, that feels so good."

"Let me make you feel better, let me do it all," he says after pulling away from my breast. His lips are shiny and he kisses me on the lips once more before working his way down, shimmying his body on the couch as well to give himself room. His fingers find the waistband of my panties and pull them down over my ankles before tossing them on the ground.

He stills for a moment and my heart stops, wondering why, but he just grins and rubs his palm against his erection. "I'm all clear by the way, thought we'd get that out before things escalated. Didn't mean to ruin the moment."

I almost laugh, but I commend him for bringing it up because I completely forgot to as well. We were always safe in the past and were both clear, but years have passed, and I don't blame him if he moved on in the intimacy department with other people.

"I am too. And I'm actually on birth control now. I didn't think to pack any condoms though…"

"Me either." He winces, biting his lip. "We can stop once we get to that point if that makes you more comfortable."

He's sweet to offer that, but there isn't anything I'd like more than for him to fuck me. And knowing we're both clear and I'm on birth control is turning my mind into mush and decisions are based solely on desire.

"I want you in every way, Graham. I trust you and I hope you trust me too. Let's do it."

"Yes, ma'am," he replies with a grin before I grab his head full of hair again, this time with both hands as he leans back down and spreads my thighs with his large hands.

His tongue is instantly on my clit, and my hips buck at the movement, sensitivity and pleasure sparking throughout my body.

"Oh, God!" I moan out, unable to contain it.

Graham only grunts and groans in response as he continues to make circles with his tongue before slipping in between my folds. I squeal from the intrusion and can already feel myself getting closer to climax. It's almost embarrassing how fast I'm ready to finish with just his tongue on me.

"Relax, Sugarplum." He chuckles from below, and I tug his hair a bit to shut him up. This seems to do the trick as he continues to lap his tongue at my entrance, and then he adds a finger…or is that two? Either way, it makes me squirm underneath him, and I can't keep the moans at bay. He seems to be enjoying it since he adds another finger and thrusts them at an even pace before quickening it.

"I'm so close," I gasp, unable to concentrate on anything anymore. I throw my head back, stars in my eyes as I hear him mumble something like *come for me, baby* and my world crashes down as I finish all over his fingers and mouth. He slips his fingers out of me slowly before shifting on the couch to hover above me.

He places kisses on my cheeks and then my lips, smirking the whole time. "You sure you're up for more?"

I roll my eyes with what energy I have left and nod, lifting my palm to wrap around his throat gently. "I didn't say to stop, Frosty."

His brow raises before he laughs. "Bold statement, Paloma." His words come out in a deeper octave and it sends shivers down my spine. He starts to pull off his boxers, tossing them to God knows where, and I lick my lips, unable to wait for more.

I need him badly and I think he needs me just as much by the way his eyes light up under the fire's glow. He spits in his hand before rubbing it up and down his length, leaning down as I shift my body so he can place his tip near my entrance. My body instantly reacts to that touch alone and I squirm.

"Easy, baby," he whispers before pushing his tip in slowly. His length enters me inch by inch, and I gasp at the feeling. I forgot how *good* he feels and I consume him in every way. He pushes until he's at the hilt, and I wrap my legs around his waist. His hips move back a bit before he thrusts forward, and I let out a sound I've never made before. He just chuckles and continues to move, causing me to throw my head back again and again, a goner for him.

The couch creaks from the movements as he speeds up and I get profusely louder and ready to release once more.

"You feel so good," I let out in sparse breaths. He groans, thrusting into me a few more times before moving his palm directly over my lower belly.

"You take me so well, baby. I can feel myself right here," he says, pressing his palm down for a moment and it makes me moan. Nothing prepares me for the release and how wet I get in this moment.

"Fuck," I gasp, shutting my eyes.

"You're so wet. Keep coming, baby. I want to feel you all over me," he lets out breathlessly while thrusting even faster. It only takes a few more thrusts before I'm finishing again and he does too, pulling out in time and letting it drip on my belly.

"I'm going to pass out," he groans, half collapsing on me and attempting to hold himself up on the couch. I let my legs fall before I wrap my arms around him and tug until his whole body-weight is on me.

"Let me catch my breath." I laugh. We stay like this for a moment, our bodies moving together with each breath. Our skin molded as one.

It's not until the fireplace makes a noise that we both seem to snap back to reality. He clears his throat and leans up. I expect him to just get off me and resume things as usual, but he kisses my lips and then my forehead before slowly getting up.

"I'll get a towel to clean you up and then I'll fix the fire so it keeps burning throughout the night." He pulls on his boxers and runs his hand through his hair as he stands tall. I smile and nod.

"We can't forget about our tea before bedtime," I remind him.

He chuckles and nods. "We'll need the sleep. We have that last song to write for Colbie and Montrose."

Right, the songs. For a moment, I forgot why we're really here. We have everything done but the last song.

The love duet.

Graham

CHAPTER SIXTEEN

I WAKE up with a sore body and the feeling of a cold coming on. Fuck, this can't be happening. There's also the smell of the last bits of wood still trying to burn in the fireplace, almost gone out.

I groan, pulling myself up and rubbing my eyes with the back of my hands. There's a soft moan behind me and arms pulling me back down. I let out an *oof* as I collide with Paloma. She giggles as I turn my head to see her smiling wide with sleepy eyes.

"Sleep well?" I ask, rolling my body so we're face-to-face. She stretches her leg over my hip, and I grab onto her thigh, steadying her. The blankets are entangled in our legs. Her face is content as she yawns and nods.

"Very well, actually. Didn't even feel cold…" She opens her eyes fully before continuing, "but now I definitely feel it. The fire went out, didn't it?"

I lean in closer and brush my nose against hers. "Not completely, but it's starting to die out. I was just about to get up and add more wood to it."

"My frosty hero," she hums, moving her nose side to side to

brush against my lips. I smile and open my mouth, fake biting her with a snapping sound before she leans back and giggles. "No!"

"We haven't made those sugar cookies we bought at the grocery store. But you're definitely tastier," I tease, leaning in again toward her nose. She tilts her neck, and I dive in, giving her a love bite on her covered shoulder.

"Or you could just kiss me again," she whispers. I lift my head to look at her and almost melt at the sight.

"I feel a cold coming from all this weather change. I don't want to get you sick. Plus, what if I have horrible morning breath and you've been too nice to say anything?"

She shrugs. "That's a normal part of every person's morning. So, what? And if you get me sick, it's not like it wouldn't have happened regardless. I have the immune system of a leaf."

A laugh bubbles out of me. "What does that even mean?"

"That's the point! You don't know. *I* don't know. But I get sick at the most inopportune times because I have the worst immune system."

"Of a leaf," I repeat, laughing again. She joins in and I cherish this moment for as long as I can before I remember the fire dying. "I must get up," I tell her, unwrapping myself from her and the blankets.

She pouts and it breaks my heart. "But we're so cozy."

"And we're about to be freezing if I don't," I remind her before giving her one last kiss on the forehead and then getting up.

She pulls the blankets back over her body and shimmies into the warmth. I give her one last glance before I head to the fireplace to assess what I need to do next to keep it going.

"WE NEED it to be cheesy with lots of holiday terms," Paloma states, tapping her gel pen against her journal in one hand and flipping her purple pick in the other.

"No, no. We have to make it mean something." I lean back on the couch with my guitar against my chest and I strum a few chords we've been working with.

"So no *Frosty* or *Sugarplums*, got it," she hums before crossing out those words in her journal. I smile and strum the chords again.

"Okay, that would be cute in a way. I won't say no to those ideas just yet."

Paloma looks up from her journal with a wide grin. "I think it'll fit for us as songwriters too. It'll be from the heart."

I strum the guitar a bit more and a verse comes to mind. "*The snow is falling thick and slow, outside our window pane.*"

Paloma starts to write down what I sing, then adds her own flair. "*The radio is playing carols low, the ones we'd used to sing.*"

"*We might be feet away but it feels worlds apart,*" I add.

She taps her pen against the journal for a moment before she glances at me and sings, "*Tell me you feel the same in your cold and Frosty heart.*"

"Whoa!" I interrupt, laughing. She leans her head back in a fit of giggles before writing it down in her journal.

"It's a good one, right?"

"I think you need to change that Frosty to Sugarplum!"

She shakes her head. "Not happening. It wouldn't rhyme or flow as well."

I roll my eyes before smirking. "Fine, keep it. But I get to make the verse with Sugarplum in it."

She taps the end of the pen on her chin before her eyes get bright. "What if we called it Second Verse?"

"That doesn't scream holiday duet," I counter. "I want it to be known on the EP track list."

"True," she says before biting her lip. "Let's finish the chorus and see if that has a good title mixed into it."

"Sounds good to me, Sugarplum," I say, pulling myself back to a sitting position with my guitar and winking at her. Her cheeks get red and my heart warms at the sight.

This Frosty is definitely wanting a second verse with Sugarplum, that's for sure.

BY THE TIME we finish writing the chorus and then the rest of the verses and bridge needed, we have a song, and most importantly, a finished EP.

We took a break to eat lunch and rest in the hot tub while the sun was shining, melting more of the snow and ice, before we decided to record the voice memo for Montrose.

My phone rings as Paloma starts to pull her hair into a ponytail. It's Montrose, so I pick it up and put him on speaker. "Hey, with Paloma."

"How are you guys? Thanks for keeping me up to date on that snowstorm," Montrose says. I made sure to send him texts here and there so he knew we were okay. I'm not sure if Paloma did at all, so I wanted my bases covered so Montrose didn't send out search and rescue for us.

"Of course, the sun is out today, so I'm hopeful everything will melt so I can shovel the driveway and get us out of here."

Montrose clears his throat. "So that means the EP is done? You guys did it?"

Paloma is the one to respond this time, leaning in. "Yep! We did it. Took some effort and a few fights, but Frosty here pulled through."

I almost tickle her for that, but I hold back. "Frosty?" Montrose calls over the phone.

"She means me. She's been hellbent on that nickname since

the start of this work trip, Montrose," I chime in. He laughs over the speaker.

"Alright, well, I'm glad it all worked out despite the snowstorm. Colbie said she loved the memos you sent so far."

"Really?" Paloma and I say at the same time. We smile before tuning into Montrose.

"So much so that she is ready to start recording them. She's got her band rehearsing right now, actually."

"No way!" Paloma exclaims, her smile spreading even further from ear to ear.

"Believe it," Montrose replies happily. I can practically feel his smile through the phone. "This is going to be so good for not just the label but you two."

That's when things get quiet, and Paloma and I glance at each other. Right, our separate songwriting contracts. My chest feels heavy for a moment and I try to ground my thoughts by counting to ten slowly in my mind.

"That's great," Paloma finally speaks up.

"So awesome," I manage to let out.

Our contracts are still active for a bit, so there's nothing we can do about it. There's nothing I can do to change the past. But that doesn't mean we can try to patch things up in the meantime. I've got all the time in the world for Paloma.

"Great, well, I'll let Colbie know about the last song being done, and please make it back safely to the airport. I'll have her jet ready to take you back, y'all let me know when."

"Sounds good," Paloma says while I let out a "I'll let you know."

Montrose hangs up the call, and we rest back on the couch. Paloma stretches her arm out, fingers twiddling in the air. I look at her, and she smiles. I lean over and intertwine her fingers with mine. Enclosing my hand in hers.

"Almost back to reality," she whispers.

"This can be our new reality," I remind her, hoping she will think about it. Not a relationship, but rekindling what we had and going from there. I want to do it right this time.

"The outside pressure won't be too much?"

I shake my head. "Not if we let it be."

"That's so easy for you to say, Graham. It's going to be tough going back to how things were, you know."

"I'm not asking to go back to that. I'm asking for another chance to prove to you that I am no longer that arrogant boy you knew before."

Paloma's lips turn into a small smile. "We have contracts to go back to. Songs to write *alone*."

I shrug. "We don't have to write together for our label. Let us just write for *us*."

"You realize Lacey won't forgive you as easily as me, right?"

I nod, knowing full well that Lacey will be the hardest to get to be okay with this. *Us*. The only one I think would be happy about this is Stetson. "I'll do my best to get her on my sweet side again."

She laughs at that as I pull her by the hand and she squeals before colliding in my arms. We hold each other for a moment, and I close my eyes, breathing her in. I'm going to miss this cabin and this week with Paloma. Guess Barney wasn't wrong about it being a magical town.

Frostpine Hollow found a way to work its magic on Paloma and I and I think that is a true Christmas miracle.

I kiss the top of her head, and she snuggles deeper into me, so I let myself relax—before I know it, I'm fast asleep with Paloma in my arms.

Paloma

CHAPTER SEVENTEEN

LACEY PULLS me in for a hug the moment I get home, and I let her shake me a bit with her excitement.

"How did it go?!" She pulls back, her eyes are gleaming with interest.

I bring my luggage and guitar case inside, head to the living room, and Lacey is quick to follow. Ferris watches me from the mantle as I place my guitar case on the couch and the luggage on the floor.

"It went better than expected. A bit rocky at first, but the songs were written."

Lacey squeals and claps her hands. "I'm so happy for you, Songbird! I knew you could do it. How was the Grinch?"

I laugh at that. "Well, he's *Frosty* now and he was bearable. More than that, Lacey."

She raises a brow. "Oh? Tell me," she says before grabbing my hand and leading me to the couch to sit us both down. She's wearing a cozy grey pajama set, and I can't wait for our movie night she planned for us while texting her on the plane.

Graham let me know that he'd be with Stetson for a bit, but if I needed him to come over, he could. We had to see each other in the studio tomorrow anyway to work with Colbie on the songs to make sure everything went smoothly, so I told him I'd just see him then. I missed my best friend anyway, and popcorn with Valentina was calling my name.

"He's different. A good different."

Her brows scrunch together. "Really? Graham Westin? The cocky songwriter? Did you hit your head in the mountains?"

I laugh and shake my head. "No, no. I'm fine, really. But I think having this work trip *and* being snowed in with him helped me get to know him better. The real him minus the Nashville glow."

"And what is the real him like? You have to remember how things ended, Paloma. I'm not saying I'm not happy for you, but I want to be the friend who sticks by you through thick and thin. And that means making sure you're not wearing rose-colored glasses after being snowed in with your ex."

"I get that, and I love you for it. But, really, it felt different this week. Like we were able to really talk about how things ended. He definitely had things to say, and trust me, he's learned his lesson."

"So are you planning to get back together or be friends?"

"I think the mature thing we can do is be friends while trying to see if we truly are meant to get back together."

"As long as he's only doing it with you, then I'll hold back my protectiveness."

I pull her in for a hug, and she squeezes me before leaning back. "I know you'll defend my honor the moment you need to, Lace."

"You betcha, Songbird. You need to play at Sparrow's again, maybe some of the new songs you've written?"

"From the EP?" I ask.

"No," she laughs, "I know you were able to write some songs for yourself while there. Don't lie to me."

It's my turn to laugh as a blush creeps up my cheeks. "I did.

Some were sad, but I've got a new idea stirring in the back of my mind."

She claps her hands and gets up from the couch, reaching her hands out to help me up. "Perfect, let's get you a spot this weekend, and you get to finishing that song. But first, movies and popcorn. I've missed our Palace nights."

Palace nights. It was something we coined long ago when we realized how much we loved watching movies together in the comfort of our house. Big cozy blankets, tons of snacks, and a great movie. It helps that Palace is just a term we created by combining our names.

"I'll go change," I tell her before grabbing my stuff and heading to my room.

"LOVED the songs and the work we did today, y'all. Country radio is going to want them playing nonstop, and the fans are gonna love it," Colbie says to us as we leave the studio. Graham thanks her and I do too, a little more excited than I intended before she heads out.

Stetson joined in briefly to help her figure out a harmony before giving us a thumbs up and leaving the studio. It's nice to see him again after so long. Even though he would come over sometimes throughout the years to see Lacey, it never felt the same after the breakup.

"I can't believe we just finished an EP with *the* Colbie Brooks," I exclaim, unable to wipe the grin off my face.

He lets out a breath. "We did it." I nod as we continue to walk through the publishing studio and head outside. Nashville is finally starting to get the winter weather we had up in Frostpine Hollow, and we're decked out in scarves and big coats today. I wrap my scarf a bit tighter around my neck as he takes my hand.

"What's next?" I ask, turning to look at him. The sounds of the city are all around us, but I focus on him.

His green eyes stay on mine and his cheeks and ears are starting to get red from the cold. Like Rudolph. "Maybe a hot chocolate? Ice skating?"

"Are you asking me out, Graham?" I giggle.

"Absolutely, Paloma. Would you care for a hot chocolate and then ice skating?"

I nod, grinning. "I'd love that, Frosty."

He bounces a little like a happy child before grabbing my waist with his other hand. "Kiss me, Sugarplum. Make me the happiest man in the world."

"You got it, Frosty." I giggle before pushing on my tiptoes, wrapping my arms around his neck and diving in for a kiss.

I feel him instantly melt under my touch and my heart swells. He pulls back for a moment to catch his breath before he slips out, "You've always had my heart, Paloma. Thank you for giving me this second chance."

"Is this a good time to say it could be our *second verse*?" I giggle.

He rolls his eyes before peppering me with kisses all over my face and neck. "We're not using that as a song title! That's final!"

"Fine, fine, Frosty. Just kiss me again."

He picks me up a bit in his arms to twirl us, and I squeal as he holds me tightly. "Yes, ma'am."

Graham

EPILOGUE

ONE YEAR LATER

I PULL the door open for Paloma to walk through before following into the bar. It's like time hasn't passed, yet so much has changed since the last time we were here.

"Y'all are back!" Barney's voice booms throughout the space, and Paloma grabs my hand before pulling us quickly to the counter. The bar isn't too crowded since it's still daylight out and there is the faint sound of Christmas music playing in the background.

"We had to come back right where it started," Paloma tells him. His eyes flicker from her to me with the biggest smile on his face. His eyes look a bit more tired, his hair a little more white if that were even possible in a year's time.

"I heard the songs on the radio," Barney exclaims and wiggles his brows.

"Guess what she wanted to call that one?" I tease, and Paloma giggles before trying to jab me with her elbow. I move just in time to miss it.

Barney waves his hand. "Regardless, I love it. And you two are doing good?"

We both nod, and Paloma speaks up. "We're doing better than ever. Almost done with my contract and then I'll go where the wind takes me."

"And you?" Barney looks at me.

I reach over to rub the small of her back and she relaxes under my touch. "I'm just following her. She's my wind. My North Star."

Barney's eyes sparkle. "I like the sound of that. Welcome back to Frostpine Hollow. The mountain town of magic. Were you guys wanting a drink?"

"Sure," Paloma states before pulling out a barstool and plopping on it. I do the same and give him a nod.

"Can an old man request a karaoke song?" he asks, bringing us the drinks we had a year ago. The fact that he remembered our orders is remarkable. I can barely remember what I had for breakfast today.

"What are you feeling?" I ask, taking a sip of the beer he hands me. Paloma does the same once she gets her drink.

"How about *Two Red Bows*?"

I sigh dramatically, but Paloma just bounces a little in her seat. "We can do that one. It's our favorite, isn't it, Frosty?"

I squeeze her and she writhes under me. "Yeah, we can do it for you, Barney."

"Perfect!" He smiles brightly, and we finish our drinks before we hop off our seats and head to the small stage. The crowd is minimal, but I don't care. Being here with Paloma in the small town that brought us together a year ago is all that matters to me. And singing this song for Barney, I guess.

He's beaming like a little kid on Christmas morning, and I give him a nod across the bar before the song cues up. Paloma and I grab the mics and wait for the first verse to roll out before we sing.

Our love duet.

THE END

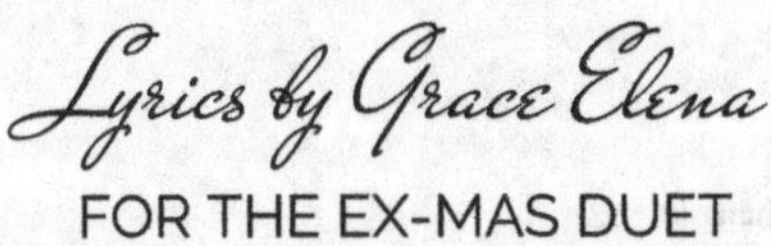

FOR THE EX-MAS DUET

NEED YOU LIKE THIS

WRITTEN BY PALOMA GENTRY-TAPIA AND GRAHAM WESTIN

No Capo

C Am F C G

V1:

It's been months since I last saw you

And by the way your hair's gotten longer

You could say that I missed you

Can't lie that you only made me stronger

Pre-Chorus:

Em Am

It's time I can't take back

But if you got the chance

Chorus:

C Am F C G

Say you need me too

It's all I need to hear from you

Say my voice brings you near

You fall to your knees when you hear

Am F C

You say you're just a mess

But I need you like this

V2:

You're unsure if I have changed

It's in the way your eyes go estranged

If only I had veered that path

You wouldn't be held under this wrath

CROSSROADS

WRITTEN BY GRAHAM WESTIN

Capo 4

Em C

V1:

I don't think Iike

The way we're so stuck on this high

Tried so hard to forget you

But it just turned my heart blue

Chorus:

Am Em/Am Em C

And you say we're fine

To walk on this dangerous line

And my heart's on fire

It's at a crossroads I cannot define

V2:

I don't think it's fair

To say I never cared

It's impossible to write down

All the feelings kept around

End chorus:

There's times I thought I'd hate you

But it's just not true…

TENNESSEE SMOKESHOW

WRITTEN BY GRAHAM WESTIN

Capo 2

Bm G D Am

V1:

Heaven only feels this good

when I'm looking in your eyes

Hell is the place where I would

go if I ever said bye

Chorus:

I've got a few words for you darling

Don't take this for granted

What happened to your eyes sparkling

It's what got me enchanted

You're a Tennessee Smokeshow, baby

Radiant piece of art

You're a Tennessee Smokeshow, baby

That's from my heart

from my heart.

V2:

I only feel this kind of peace

when you're holding me tight

Kiss me for some kind of release

it's only you on my mind

MUSIC OR ME

WRITTEN BY PALOMA GENTRY-TAPIA

Capo 3

C Em Am F

V1:

I don't know what I'm doing here

But I'll take it as a sign

Do you remember all my fears?

Wish it was easy to rewind

V2:

We fall back like never before

Do you feel this pull too?

Everytime I see that damn door,

Brings me back to when I lost you

Chorus:

Is it the music or me?

That brought our misery?

Should we take this chance, baby?

To rewrite our destiny

V3:

You hold all the cards,

When I once was your Queen

I've been left with these scars

But you'll never feel what I mean

Bridge:

I hate the way, you look at me

From across the room, I can't look away

I hate the way, you loved me

You made me bloom, then pushed me away

UNDER THIS MISTLETOE

WRITTEN BY PALOMA GENTRY-TAPIA AND GRAHAM WESTIN

Capo 3

D G D G

V1:

Santa might be coming down his way

But I know I've got no present on his sleigh

The bells are ringing loud and clear tonight

No reason to stay awake through the night

Chorus:

Em G D Am

I'm checking you once, twice, three times

Santa can't stop this wish of mine

So come on over, it's something you already know

And get yourself under this mistletoe

Under this mistletoe

V2:

These cookies and milk are getting cold

Cause my heart ain't a heart of gold

Santa knows I'm on the naughty list

Yet he wraps you around my mind in a twist

COLD DECEMBER

WRITTEN BY PALOMA GENTRY-TAPIA

Capo 2 Am F G Em

V1:

All I want for Christmas is you

Playing on the jukebox in this room

And all i can stand to do, is look at you

V2:

Don't tell me that you've gone and changed

It's clear that I'm the only one here to blame

And all I can stand to say, is turn the other way

Chorus:

fa la la la la

You went breaking my heart

In the dead of winter

Do you even remember

Fa la la la la

now all I have are these scars

From the way you splinter

now it's just a cold December

V3:

I can see a ghost in those green eyes

You've been hiding all your truths and your lies

And all I can stand to compromise, is to hear your honest cries

Bridge:

and you thought

That you could

Get away with so much and more

And I fought

to be understood

Not pushed away and left and bruised and sore

TWO RED BOWS

WRITTEN BY PALOMA GENTRY-TAPIA AND GRAHAM WESTIN

Capo 4

D G A D

V1:

The snow is falling thick and slow, outside our window pane

The radio is playing carols low, the ones we'd used to sing

We might be feet away, but it feels worlds apart

Tell me you feel the same in your cold and Frosty heart?

Chorus:

I've got the presents under the tree, for you and for me

There's hot cocoa the way you like, extra sweet

There's just one red bow in my hand tonight

But if you come over it'll be two red bows tonight

V2:

Now the snow is melting slowly, with the season's change

The radio only reminds me of the time you walked away

Now we're world's apart, baby, come be near

There's a song playing in my heart, please won't you hear

Bridge:

Two red bows

Wrapped in love

Two red bows

And it's all because…

WHISKEY AND MISTLETOE

WRITTEN BY PALOMA GENTRY-TAPIA AND GRAHAM WESTIN

Capo 3

Em Am F G

V1:

You always told me

you'd leave at last snowfall

You then kissed my cheek

said you'd never call

Pre-Chorus:

This was not in my plan

This could not be where you stand

Chorus:

But Whiskey became my friend

When the nights seemed to never end

One shot, two shots, you became my foe

Three shots, guess it's not whiskey and mistletoe

V2:

Now I've got this headache

I can only blame you

The pieces of this freezing heart

Could only break in two

NORTH STAR

WRITTEN BY PALOMA GENTRY-TAPIA AND GRAHAM WESTIN

Capo 4

C Em Am F

V1:

When I was lost

You found me

Thought there was no trust

But you showed me

Yeah, you showed me

Chorus:

You are

The one for me

My North Star

Always guiding me

Home

You are… my home

V2:

I'd do the same

If you ever need

If you lost direction

Take my hand and see

Yeah and see

SANTA GOT ME A GIBSON

WRITTEN BY PALOMA GENTRY-TAPIA AND GRAHAM WESTIN

Capo 2

C F Am G

V1:

All I want for Christmas

Are some brand new boots

Doesn't have to be a Stetson

Tecovas will do

Pre-Chorus:

But I guess he don't know

The main thing I want

he's up at the North Pole

So here's what I want:

Chorus:

A lovely mahogany

Gibson guitar

It's all that I need

It'll take me far

I thought he'd

Never listen

But turns out…

Santa got me a Gibson

V2:

All I want for Christmas

Is a horse or two

Doesn't have to be a mustang

A Belgian will do

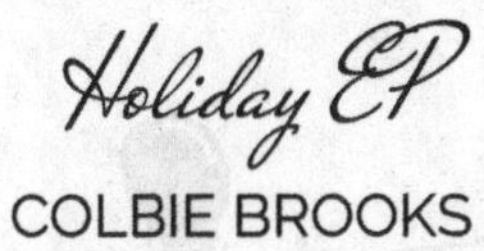

COLBIE BROOKS

WHISKEY AND MISTLETOE

1. Under This Mistletoe

2. Santa Got Me A Gibson

3. Two Red Bows (ft. Irving Holland)

4. North Star

5. Whiskey and Mistletoe

*Written by Paloma Gentry-Tapia and Graham Westin

*Produced by Brooks Row Records and Indigo Roots Publishing

Coming Soon by Grace Elena

TENNESSEE ROOTS UNIVERSE

Alpine Ridge Series

Sweet Like Brittle

Book 2

Acknowledgments

Thank you for reading this novella that took shape in my head, and heart, for a bit now. I've been wanting to write a book solely based on songwriting MC's and this was just it. Thank you for taking a chance on it, dear reader.

There are a few people I'd love to thank while I worked hard to publish my *seventh* novel.

To Lizzie, thank you for being my rock and constantly providing the support and PA needs that I don't even know I need sometimes. I cherish you every day and I am still so excited for the day we can finally meet in person. It will happen very soon, trust. You have always picked up the pieces when my creativity died out, created the best graphics to market my books, and kept a steady place to fall to when author things got too much. Thank you.

To Kassidy, thank you for always being there for my crazy ideas. Thank you for hearing me out via text on this wild idea that transpired through my hundreds of hours of binging *Nashville* and wanting to write something so random and so quick that you just said *yes*. Thank you for working out the kinks with me. This novella's backbones are fortified by you.

To Shelby, thank you for always supporting and shouting your love from the rooftops. I appreciate you so much for always standing in my corner since those Wattpad days. Look at us now. Wow. I love you and can't wait for the day we meet and get sodies.

To my hometown friends, thank you for being here through

the thick and thin, the different eras that we've seen each other since we were 15. Adna, Karla, and Sandy—I love y'all so much and I can't wait to continue thriving in our friendships until we're gray and old.

To my besties Emily and Kelsey, thank you for believing in me and always being there for adult Grace when she's not Grace Elena. I am who I am because of our friendship and I love you both so much. Your support means the world to me. Thank you for being here on this wild ride with me.

To my editor and author friend, Cassidy, thank you for all you do. You are a dear friend that I hope will be there for all the years to come. Seeing you flourish as an author and editor has been the best thing and I appreciate you so much as both a colleague/client and as a friend.

To my brothers, I appreciate all your support even if you have no idea what I write. Let's keep it that way. Thank you for having my books on your shelf. For believing in me. And for being there states away.

To my parents, thank you for the love and devotion to not just each other but to me. I write love that I've grown to see. Love is kind, patient, challenging, has its curves, and it's you two. Growing up seeing your kind of love and the sacrifices made is inspirational. Thank you for also letting me chase my dreams even if it meant moving 8 hours away all alone to Nashville, TN when I was just 17. It was scary, but life changing. Like I said in the author's note, I might've not gotten my Broadway moment or Opry debut, but this is close enough. And this isn't the last. Thank you for constantly loving me through the phases, the growth, the mistakes, and the hardships.

To Milo, I hope you're still looking down happily seeing me type away the kind of found family and friendships that you've shown me years ago. I love you.

To my honey, thank you for showing me the kind of love that I write about. I thought I had it right once, but you're more.

About the Author

Grace Elena is a Mexican American author who loves to write slow burn romances with strong Latinx leads. She's been writing since she could remember and even dabbled in some songwriting during her college years. When Grace isn't writing, she's spending time with her cat in Nashville, Tennessee.

If you like more forbidden romances, Grace writes under another pen name G. Elena. Check out those books for more spice and more fun!

Visit her website at graceelenaauthor.com or you can keep up with her on Instagram @graceelenaauthor and @gelenaauthor.

If you'd like to have more insight to her books before anyone else, join her Private Facebook Group "Grace Elena's Vineyard."